BITTERSWEET STORM

BITTERSWEET STORM

JANIS HARRISON

DOUBLEDAY & COMPANY, INC.
GARDEN CITY, NEW YORK
1985

All of the characters in this book
are fictitious, and any resemblance
to actual persons, living or dead,
is purely coincidental.

Library of Congress Cataloging in Publication Data
Harrison, Janis.
Bittersweet storm.
I. Title.
PS3558.A6713B5   1985   813′.54
ISBN 0-385-23056-7
Library of Congress Catalog Card Number 85-10424

CHAPTER ONE

With an angry swipe of my hand, I brushed the pile of bills off the table. They fluttered to the threadbare carpet like leaves on a crisp fall morn. It was a senseless action. Knocking them to the floor hadn't gotten rid of them. I still owed the money.

I didn't bother looking at the names. I knew them by heart. I tossed the gathered debts on the table and walked to the window. Outside was the bustling city of St. Louis, Missouri. I would never get used to city life. I wanted to be back out in the country, away from all the noise and the crowds of people.

Going home was impossible. I turned from the window with a sigh. My glance circled the drab room, coming to rest on the mirror over the wash table. What I saw failed neither to surprise nor to please me. I thought the last eight months might have shown on my face. I looked the same. My slender face was haggard. Dark ugly circles did nothing to complement my green eyes. As always, my thick auburn hair was escaping its hairpins. Wisps floated lazily around my face and ears. On another woman it might have been flattering. Maybe even sensuous. On me it looked unkempt.

I stood up straight and placed my hands at my narrow waist. Taking a deep breath, I watched the swell of my breasts. I nodded my head in satisfaction. "Not bad," I murmured. I released my pent-up air in a hiss of dejection. Who would see me here? With a wry twist of my lips, I added, Do I want to be seen in my faded dress and run-over shoes?

It was hard to believe that only a few short months ago I might have been getting dressed in my fine clothes to receive afternoon visitors at my beloved home. The only home I'd ever known. Willowcrest. Just thinking the name filled me with a longing that was like a physical blow.

I closed my eyes, seeing Willowcrest in my mind. Made of gray native stone, it was a sight to behold. The large two-story house sat atop a knoll overlooking the Mississippi River. Century-old willow trees acted as sentinels, guarding us over the years. From the house, as far as the eyes could see was fertile land. Crestwood land.

I slowly opened my eyes. I had to correct myself. Not Crestwood land any longer. Willowcrest belonged to another. With the ill-fated turn of a card, my father had lost it all. The house, acres of farm ground, cattle, even the buggies and horses had been gambled and lost.

I'd been over and over it in my mind, but it was always the same. We, my father and I, were homeless, depending on Hilda's kindness and generosity. Hilda was a distant cousin of my mother's, but I loved her. I knew it didn't bother Hilda having us living above her millinery store. But it bothered me. I knew it was an added burden to have me and Papa depending on her, but what could I do?

Papa needed me to care for him. He was dreadfully ill. I didn't have time to find a job. Instead I kept busy here at the store. I cooked the meals. I cleaned the store and the upstairs rooms. My back ached and my fingers grew numb from helping with the extra sewing. Hilda's shop was doing very well. It kept her busy, but the income didn't stretch far enough to include two extra people, especially one who was in need of medical attention.

I tiptoed to the open door and peeked in at Papa. He'd always been a big handsome man. Now he was a skeleton of his old self. Each day he seemed to shrink until he was only skin and bones. The doctor had diagnosed his condition as critical and his ailment a disease of the lungs.

Tears came to my eyes. I didn't need to be told. Papa was

dying. For his sake I could only feel relief. I knew he was suffering. It hurt me to see him in pain. Struggling for each breath he took. In death he would be free. But how was I to find my freedom? I adored Papa. He was all I had now that my home was gone. I didn't want to be left alone.

When Mama had died, I had turned more and more to Papa, as he had to me. We grew close. But I knew I hadn't been able to fill that special void Mama's death had left. At first the gambling had been an outlet for his loneliness. As time passed I noticed certain possessions missing from the house. They weren't of value. A vase here. A picture there. Until I had become concerned. When confronted with my worries, Papa had looked ashamed. I didn't think I'd ever forget the look of embarrassment on his face. He explained his run of bad luck and overdrawn bank account. He was using some of the possessions as a deposit for his debts. He vowed to stop when they were taken care of. I believed him. I didn't belittle or criticize. I stood by his side. For a while his promise held true. Never had we been closer. I don't know what set off his gambling again. He began staying out all night. He lost weight and became edgy and preoccupied.

When I tried talking to him, he just patted me on the head, like he used to do when I was a child. It was about this time his cough worsened. All of these things worried me, but I hadn't an inkling that my happy life was fast coming to an end.

Nine months ago, Papa called me into his study. He tried to cushion the blow, but the situation was out of his hands. He had lost it all. We had one month to pack up our personal belongings and be gone from Willowcrest.

I had remained brave while in Papa's study. It was later when I was alone that I let myself go. My heart was broken. I hadn't asked any questions. He'd told me all I could take in at the time. Everything was gone. Even the bed, where I'd thrown myself to weep out my grief, belonged to another.

"Grant Whitmore." The very name tasted bitter on my

tongue. I clasped my hands in anger. He had stolen everything from us. Taking advantage of Papa's obvious sickness, Whitmore had picked him clean. I abhorred the man. I prayed I would never set eyes on him. I couldn't be held responsible for what I might say or do to him.

Willowcrest had been in the Crestwood family for over five generations. It had never belonged to another. Now it was in the hands of a stranger. Such a loathsome man. A gambler. No! He wasn't just a gambler, like Papa had been, Whitmore was a professional. He made his living on the riverboats, fleecing others of their worth.

God, I moaned softly under my breath. Why couldn't he have stayed on the boat? Instead he had gotten off at St. Louis, taking up residence at the Grand Hotel. It was there that Papa had made Whitmore's acquaintance. It had been a costly meeting. Not just because of Willowcrest, but the late-night prowling and added worry had aggravated his illness.

A raspy cough from the bedroom interrupted my recollections. I used the corner of my apron to wipe the traces of my tears away. I forced a pleasant smile to my lips and walked into Papa's room.

My smile slipped as I bent to place a kiss to his pale cheek. He felt feverish. His eyes looked unusually bright as they darted here and there around the room. I wondered if I should go for the doctor.

"How are you feeling, Papa?" I asked gently.

He opened his mouth to speak but coughed. The cough rattled deep in his chest. He gasped for breath. I helped him sit higher in bed, then poured a glass of water.

"Drink this. Don't try to talk. Just rest."

He took a drink while I fluffed his pillows and smoothed the covers on the bed. He caught my hand in his and pulled me down beside him.

"Don't fuss, sweetheart," he whispered.

"I'm not fussing, Papa. I just want to make you comfortable.

Relax," I said soothingly. "I'll do the talking. Something very funny happened downstairs this morning." I started to tell him, but he shook his head.

"Not now, Althea. I have something to discuss. When you were born, your mother and me had such high hopes for you. We loved you dearly and wanted only the best for you. Now I'm leaving you with nothing." He stopped talking to take a deep breath. Inhaling caused him to cough.

I smiled at him. "Don't talk, Papa. Money doesn't matter," I lied. If it would help him rest easier, I'd tell him anything. "I'm far richer than you think. I've had a happy life. When you're better we'll leave St. Louis. We'll go make our fortunes somewhere else."

He shook his head sadly. "Don't coddle me, Daughter. I know I'm dying. You know it too. For once in my life, I've been very practical. I have something to tell you. I wanted it to come from me." He stopped to catch his breath and steady his rapid breathing. He couldn't die in peace until he knew he'd tried to prepare Althea for what was to come.

He wiped his mouth with a trembling hand. His eyes held a look of apprehension. "This isn't easy to say, my dear. I want you to know I've had your best interests at heart. I'd hoped to see my grandchildren before I die, but that isn't to be." His voice trailed away weakly. His eyes closed wearily.

I was puzzled. I didn't know what Papa was talking about. But I was frightened. He looked afraid of my reaction. What had he done? I tried to put my own fears aside. "Don't talk, Papa. Save your strength. Maybe later you'll feel more like talking."

He struggled to open his eyes. His voice was low and reedy. "I knew this would be difficult. That's why I've been putting it off. I'm dying, Daughter. I have to say it now." He saw me shaking my head and chided me. "Don't contradict me. We've had some difficult times. You stood by my side through it all.

I'm grateful. I couldn't have asked for a more forgiving daughter."

He smiled up at me and gave my hand a squeeze. "I don't know what we would have done without Hilda. She's always been a valuable friend to us. I wish I could show her our appreciation, but I don't have the money to do so."

"Papa, Hilda knows our situation. She's glad to help us. As for the money, don't worry. We're doing just fine. Mr. Whitmore was most generous in letting us take some of our more personal treasures. We could sell them if things get too bad." As I talked I could hear the hard note creep into my voice. I tried to soften my tone, but apparently I wasn't successful.

William, hearing the contempt, reprimanded me. "I know how you feel about Grant, but you'll have to get over that. It wasn't his fault. I did it all with a purpose." He smiled, seeing my obvious puzzlement. "I know this is hard for you to believe. To be truthful with you, Althea, at first it never entered my mind. I did gamble away the money with a compulsion I now find disgusting, but at the time I couldn't stop."

He was silent, remembering. I was silent, worrying. Surely Papa didn't know what he was saying. It was his sickness. He was delirious. I couldn't believe Papa had lost everything to Whitmore on purpose.

"I can see your disbelief. You think I'm making it up." He shook his head. "I'm too sick, Althea. What I'm saying will be hard for you to understand. Even harder for you to accept. I did it all for your own good. You had to be protected. I couldn't leave you without any prospects or without a home."

Then the whole story came out. Papa spoke slowly and at times his voice faded away. I often had to lean forward to hear all his words. Even then I thought I'd misunderstood him.

"Since your mother died, I've found solace in gaming parlors. I've enjoyed the noise and the excitement. Most of all, I've enjoyed meeting new and interesting people. About a year ago, I had the good fortune to meet Grant Whitmore."

Papa stopped speaking when he saw the pained expression on my face. "I know you don't see it that way, but to me it was fortunate. I worked very hard to cultivate his acquaintance. I'd heard his name mentioned many times in the months before I saw him face to face. He's made his living on the riverboat, doing well for himself. What intrigued me was his other reputation."

I found I was interested in spite of myself. I didn't want to hear about the man who stole my home, and yet the more I knew of him the better my chances would be to avenge all the wrongs he'd done us. I questioned Papa. "What other reputation? Is he a murderer? A cutthroat?" I heard the scorn in my voice.

William tried to laugh, but it was a weak croak. "My darling Daughter, don't always think the worst of the poor fellow. He has many recommendations. I'm proud of my choice. He comes from a good family. He's capable of running a large estate. He's interested in the prospering of Willowcrest. He has plenty of money of his own. But most of all, he isn't married."

I frowned. I'd been uneasy from the start of this talk. With Papa's last words, my unrest turned into fear. I asked, "Papa, what have you done?"

"I've been planning your future. You need someone to look after you. I've found the right man." As I started to get up from the bed, he feebly grabbed my arm. "Sit still," he commanded. "I have more to say. It won't meet with your approval, but it had to be done. I checked and double-checked the character of Grant Whitmore. He's an honest man. Since I'm also an honest man, I know you will honor my debt to him. You see, Althea. I lost more than Willowcrest. I've lost you as well."

I sat frozen to the bed. My own father wouldn't have used me in his poker games. I slowly shook my head. No. Papa wouldn't and yet . . . I felt my face flush with shame. What laughter and ridicule there must have been in the parlor that night. William Crestwood's plain unmarried old-maid daughter had to be won in a game of cards. My chin came up. I wouldn't go through with it. If Papa had lost his pride, I would keep mine.

I pulled my arm free of his feeble grasp to move away. I ignored the tears in my eyes and cried, "Papa, I can't believe you would bet my freedom. Tell me I've misunderstood you. I beg of you. What of my pride? My life? Am I to be sold to this man?" I laughed bitterly. "No! Oh no! I'm being given to him on a silver platter! The gambling houses must have rocked with laughter that night." Tears choked my throat, so I could barely speak. "Did your cronies find it amusing? How high did the bidding go? What is my total worth?"

My harsh words hurt Papa. I felt ashamed of my outburst, but I was hurting too. I had to strike out. I felt betrayed by a man I loved and respected.

"Daughter, no one knows of this bargain. There wasn't any jokes or laughter. This is between Grant and myself. Now you know. Gus Sawyer might have guessed what I was planning, but I never told him and he's not questioned me about this." William tried to pull himself up on one elbow so he could see me better. His breathing was ragged, but he gathered his remaining strength.

"Althea, go to the bureau. Pull out the third drawer. Stuck to the bottom is a piece of paper. It's my copy of the agreement between Grant and me. It's yours now."

I did as Papa directed. With the paper in hand, I closed my eyes, trying to sort out my feelings. Did I really want to know the provisions of their agreement? I felt the urge to rip the paper to shreds. My angry thoughts must have shown on my face.

"It won't erase the agreement if the paper is destroyed, my dear. Grant has a copy and I have another in the vault at the bank. This is for your own good, Althea." His voice cracked with emotion and strain. "Please, my dear. Don't hate me. I've not done it to hurt or shame you. I've tried to think of your own good. Marriages are arranged all the time. Often they work out better than the ones left up to chance." He stared at me, waiting for a smile. Seeing none, he lay back against the pillows, exhausted. Another spasm of coughing caused me to forget my own hurt and anger. I went to his side. Tenderly I picked up his hand.

"I love you, Papa. I don't like this and I'm not sure if I can accept it. I'm trying to believe you did it with my future in mind, but it's so drastic. I don't have to be married to have a good and happy life. I can find work and live in a room here in town. Someday if things work out, I might meet a man and fall in love. I'll go to Mr. Whitmore and explain how I feel."

"No!" he shook his head fiercely. "No. That isn't possible. As soon as I'm gone, Grant will come to claim his bride. You could run away, but what would it solve? This way you'll be living at Willowcrest. You'll have all the dresses and prestige that go with his name. 'Whitmore' is a well-known family down South. Besides, you won't be alone in the world. Grant will protect you and look after you. If you run away, Althea, or fail to honor this agreement, all I've tried to accomplish will be in vain."

I could see all this talking was sapping his strength. He was failing right before my eyes. I brushed a kiss across his cheek. My tone was reassuring, though my mind was far from made up. "Very well, Papa. I'll try to do as you wish. But right now you have to rest. We'll talk more later."

"No! No! Can't rest!" He struggled against his weakening condition. "Have to tell you about the jewels." A violent coughing spell threatened to break his fragile bones. I wiped the spittle from his blue lips and leaned near. Wheezing and choking, he muttered, "I can't die until you know about the jewels. I didn't gamble it all away. The Crestwood jewels are hidden. They are at Willowcrest. This is another important reason why you have to go there to live. I've left them for you. They're to be your security if your marriage doesn't work."

"Where are they, Papa?" I asked.

"I've hidden them well." He smiled weakly. "I couldn't take the chance they'd be found by someone other than you. I wanted to insure your happiness, Daughter. But in order to have the jewels, it'll take some time to find them. While you're looking for them, your marriage to Grant will have time to work."

"But, Papa," I started, but he didn't appear to hear me.

"I have one clue for you. I've hidden them in a place where we've found much pleasure." His eyes widened. His hand gripped mine tightly.

I sat there at his side, knowing he was leaving me. I didn't need to go for a doctor. He wanted me near. I watched him close his eyes for the last time. Gradually the muscles in his hand relaxed. I smoothed the covers over his still body and kissed his warm cheek. All too soon his warmth would be gone. I looked down at Papa. He looked like he was sleeping peacefully. A tear gathered in my eye and rolled slowly down my cheek.

I was alone. Everyone had left me. All I had was a prospective husband. A man I hated. I walked slowly to the window and stood with my face pressed against the windowpane. My eyes stared unseeingly down into the dirty cluttered alley that ran behind the shop. I was thinking back to a time almost five months ago when I'd first seen Grant Whitmore. We'd never been introduced, so my view was from a distance. He'd been sitting majestically in his carriage, his black head held at a superior angle, his sharp steely blue eyes fixed on a spot high above everyone's head. His attitude was that of a royal prince, while I, trudging along with my basket of vegetables, looked like a lowly servant. At the time, I hadn't known who he was. He looked important, commanding attention. He had mine.

My eyes were on him rather than the broken walk at my feet. I stepped on a loose stone and fell in a tangle of petticoats and carrots.

Even now my face flushed with embarrassment. I had looked up, praying no one had witnessed my ungainly tumble. I wasn't to be spared. My own green eyes encountered those same sharp blue ones. His full lips were pursed with disapproval and disgust. I could remember scrambling to my feet and tossing my chin in the air, but his carriage had moved on out of sight. Of course, when I saw his picture in the paper, I had hated his haughty airs even more. All this time I had assumed he hadn't known who I was. Now, in light of Papa's announcement, that seemed highly unlikely. The story in the paper had said he was a very eligible bachelor.

If he was such a fine catch, I asked myself, why was he in agreement with this ridiculous scheme?

I looked back at Papa. I tried not to blame him. He'd done what he thought was good for me. Could I honor his decision? Could I give it a chance to work? I remembered those cold blue eyes. I was afraid. There were the jewels to consider too. If I found them, I would leave Grant Whitmore.

To leave him was to leave Willowcrest. I hoped Whitmore was a greedy man. I might be able to entice him from Willowcrest with the jewels. I'd rather lose the jewelry than lose Willowcrest.

I wiped the tears away and stiffened my shoulders. I told Papa good-bye one more time, then went downstairs to the store. I saw Hilda was busy with a customer, so I went out the back door.

The air smelled fresh. Winter was over. Spring was here. It was a time for new beginnings. A time for everything to come back to life.

I was twenty-six years old. Time I was getting married. Even now I was classified as an old maid. But to marry a man I didn't like? All I had was Papa's word that he was suitable. What if we hated each other? I already loathed the man. I couldn't count on finding the jewels. I frowned trying to recall Papa's exact words. "Where we've found much pleasure."

I sighed heavily. We had good times all over the house and the grounds. His clue was really no clue at all. My whole future depended on finding those gems. I didn't have one idea where to begin. After I found them, I would have a lever to bargain with. Until then I could do nothing.

There were other things to think of. Papa was gone. I had to keep repeating those words to myself. Trying to accept the fact, but part of me felt sure I could go back up to his room and hear his raspy breathing. Yet I knew he was gone. I had a funeral to arrange. But still I stayed where I was.

I'd been sixteen when Mama died. She had lain at rest in the music room at Willowcrest, with bouquets of flowers around her. That wouldn't be possible for Papa, but I'd do all I could. Nagging at me was a very practical thought. Money. I tried to push it away. Papa deserved a fine service. I'd find a way.

The tinkling of the bell above the front door jarred me away from my thoughts. Hilda's customer had gone. I had to go tell her about Papa. I went inside. As I passed a mirror, I smirked at my reflection. My hair had tumbled down to hang around my face. Most of the pins were lost. No sparkle showed in my dull eyes.

Mr. Whitmore deserved what he was getting, I told myself nastily. I asked myself, Why would such a handsome man need an arranged marriage? Perhaps he was punishing himself, taking a woman who looked like me. It was a sobering thought. I felt a shiver of apprehension. Grant Whitmore was handsome in a dark, almost sinister way. But why had he agreed with Papa? Surely he could have someone that was more agreeable and far lovelier to look at. Why me?

Those questions stayed in my mind the rest of the day. It

wasn't until evening that I had a confirmation of my suspicions of Whitmore's inner character.

I had settled down at the kitchen table to have a cup of tea when I heard a deep voice coming up from downstairs. Since all of Hilda's customers were of the female gender, I took particular notice. I got up, thinking it might have to do with Papa's death. The bell rang, letting me know the visitor had gone. A few minutes later, Hilda's footsteps sounded on the stairs.

As she came into sight, I saw a worried frown on her face. The passing years had been kind to her. She was a neat woman in her late fifties. Her dark hair was pleasantly streaked with gray. Blue eyes spoke volumes of her sorrow for me and for Papa's passing. She was more of a friend than a relative. I could see she was worried about me. She knew me very well.

"Well?" I demanded. "Who was that? I suppose they wanted money."

"No. It was Mr. Whitmore's valet. He brought you a note." She hesitated for a second longer, then reluctantly passed it to me.

I knew what was on her mind. My hair might be auburn, but I had the temperament of a true redhead. So far today my grief had suppressed my fury, but if this letter said anything out of line, Hilda knew what would happen.

I could feel my lips stretch into a line of disapproval. "He hasn't wasted any time," I muttered. I had told Hilda of the agreement. She had kept her opinion to herself. Now I looked at her and said, "What do you suppose he wants?"

She shrugged. "All you can do is open it and see."

I stared at the envelope. "ALTHEA CRESTWOOD" was written in bold black letters across the front. The handwriting confirmed my suspicions. Grant Whitmore was a masterful, arrogant man. He was used to getting his own way. His letters were formed with a very firm hand. In growing irritation, I ripped open the envelope to read the following:

Dear Miss Crestwood,

I've just received word of your father's passing. I wish to express my sympathy to you. William Crestwood was a fine man. I'm sure he has informed you of our agreement. Since the marriage is agreeable, I shall make payment of any bills you might have incurred these last months. Have them ready for my valet. I'll see to payment at once. Again my sympathy to you.

Grant Whitmore

I crumpled the letter into a tight ball. How did he know the marriage was agreeable? He hadn't met or talked to me. He was a conniving man. I felt my temper flare. If he wanted to take care of the bills, good! It was small payment for all the worry he'd placed on my shoulders. I'd see to a beautiful service for Papa. I'd buy me a new dress too. I would be only too happy to have the bills ready for him. My mind was more at ease. I began to smile in satisfaction.

Hilda noted my abrupt change of mood. She looked past the surface grin to the sparkle in my eyes. "What is it, Althea?" she asked uneasily. "What do you have on your mind?"

"Sit down. I'll try to explain." I told her I wouldn't do anything wrong. As I talked, my hands worked to smooth the wrinkles from the letter. I decided I might need it as proof of Whitmore's word concerning payment. I wasn't going to be extravagant, but I wanted the service to be perfect.

While Hilda read the letter, I took out the marriage agreement. As I looked it over, the first thing I noticed was it had the style and wording of a lawyer. In essence it said that Grant Whitmore agreed to marry Althea Crestwood. No money was to exchange hands. Only the title of Willowcrest and all the furnishings. What a price I had brought. There hadn't been a game of cards. Papa had led me to believe he'd gambled everything away. But it had been only part of his plan. He had been thinking of me and my security. It stated plainly in the agreement that no one was to know of its existence. If Whitmore changed his mind and refused to marry me, he would be forced to pay me a ridiculous sum of money and I would get a half interest in the property as well. If I failed to marry Whitmore, I would be without a home and without a cent. I would also be turning against Papa's dying wish. It seemed I had much to gain by keeping Papa's bargain. My interests were protected. The paper was binding.

As I read it over a second time, a question kept recurring. The same one I'd been asking myself all day. Why had Whitmore agreed to this? I'm sure he wasn't cornered into it. I remembered his eyes and sensed no man could force Grant Whitmore to do anything. Willowcrest was an exceptional place, but was it worth a man's freedom? It all seemed wrong. Yet I had to trust Papa.

Leaning my head on my folded arms, I sighed wearily. What was I to do? Why couldn't things have continued on as they had for years? I felt Hilda's hand on my shoulder. I looked up.

"I'm fine, Hilda. I just need time to think. Everyone is rushing me. Whitmore thinks I'm agreeable, but I'm not. I feel an obligation to Papa, since he planned this. I want to live at Willowcrest again but not as Mrs. Grant Whitmore. What should I do?"

Hilda's look was full of compassion. "You don't have to decide this minute. I'm sure Mr. Whitmore won't come for you until after the funeral. Let's get through one thing at a time. Nothing should interfere with the mourning of your father. He was a fine man. He did something very unselfish for you. Cherish it and his love for you."

Her simple words heartened me. Later that night as I undressed for bed, they came back to me. I didn't have to make a decision, but I couldn't put my problems out of my mind.

I brushed my hair, letting it fall in waves down the middle of my back. Papa had always loved my long hair. It was a chore to wash and towel it dry, but I'd complied with his wishes and not had it cut.

Tonight it felt like it weighed a ton. My neck didn't feel strong enough to hold up the mass of heavy hair. I laid down the brush to stare into the mirror. In the soft lamplight, my eyes glowed green and my hair shone. I knew I wasn't beautiful. I never would be. But I wasn't ugly either. What did Mr. Whitmore think of his prospective bride?

I tried to tell myself I didn't care. If he didn't like me, he could pay me my part and I would go away. My heart ached at the thought. Leave Willowcrest? It had been unbearable when we'd left it those many months ago. Yesterday I had no hope of calling Willowcrest mine again. Today I'd been given the chance to return.

Was it worth the price I was going to pay? I shut my eyes and took a deep breath. I would take Hilda's advice. I didn't have to make up my mind tonight. Perhaps Grant Whitmore would have a change of heart. But I knew this was impossible. I crawled between the covers and closed my weary eyes.

CHAPTER TWO

Grant Whitmore ruffled my composure again the next morning. Inside the funeral home, I found everything financially taken care of. He had set no limitations in regard to the arrangements. I was relieved of one worry but found several more. He hadn't given me a chance to balk at his ideas. He assumed I'd agree, without having a thought of my own.

Would I always find myself a few steps behind him? I was

forced to admit this might be true. As I was leaving the undertaker handed me an envelope. I looked at him, puzzled, then
glanced down at the now familiar writing. By now those loops
and curls were committed to memory. There in the bright
sunshine I read my second communication from Whitmore.

It was short and to the point. He had made all the arrangements and set up an appointment for me at a dressmaker on
Twenty-Fourth Street. He had even enclosed money for the
fare across town.

I fumed in silence. I was getting very tired of the word
"arrangements." That was all I heard. Whitmore was taking
care of everything, from Papa's burial to the mourning clothes
on my back. I was so upset I almost went back to Hilda's,
forgetting about the dress. But temptation and lack of a suitable dress made me swallow my anger. I couldn't wait until I
met this man face to face. It would give me great pleasure to
tell him what I thought of him and his high-handed ways.
Once again he'd outsmarted me. I'd planned to get a dress as
an act of defiance. He'd gone so far as to choose the dress shop
for me. I forgot my anger as a wave of anticipation swept over
me. I might resent Whitmore's dictatorial manner, but I
couldn't find fault with his taste.

I spent the next two hours in my petticoat. I twisted and
turned, was poked and jabbed until I thought I would drop. I
called a halt after deciding on four dresses. All were of dark
material. Brown, black, gray and a deep mossy green.

I looked longingly at the materials that had been pushed to
one side. It had been so long since I'd touched soft expensive
silks and satins. All the colors of the rainbow lay before me, but
out of respect for Papa I would dress in the traditional colors.

As I left, I was assured a swift delivery. I thought they meant
one dress but found a large monetary reward was being offered for their speedy service. I would have all my dresses
before the funeral service at two the following day. I didn't

want to admit it, but I was impressed with Grant Whitmore's influence, or I should say the influence his money evoked.

Back at Hilda's shop, I used my own key. Black crepe around the frame of the door designated the reason for its closing. Tomorrow was the funeral. For Papa's sake, I hoped there would be a large turnout. I wanted his passing to be noted with sorrow. For myself, I would have been content to mourn him privately.

I found Hilda sewing in the workroom. Two hats lay on the table in different stages of completion. Each had been cut from black satin. Yards of heavy tulle were being carefully stitched around the crown. Hilda had been busy while I was gone.

With a sad smile, I picked up a hat and tried it on. With relief, I saw the veil fell to my shoulders. My red-rimmed eyes and tears would be well hidden from the prying eyes of the others. I looked at my somber reflection in the mirror before taking the hat off.

"Thank you, Hilda. This will be fine."

She held out the other hat. It was a twin to mine. "I made this one for me."

"Good," I said, nodding my head. "Make out a bill for your regular price. I'll see to it you get paid."

Hilda was shocked. "Oh no. Althea, this is a gift."

I knew my lips were set in their familiar lines of stubbornness. "No. You're to be paid too." I took out the letter and the rest of the money. I handed it to her. "This was waiting for me at the funeral parlor. Read it."

She read quietly, then asked, "Did you go? Will they have a dress for you?"

"Four," I said. Seeing her surprise, I added defensively, "I haven't anything decent to wear. Besides, he was the one to suggest the dressmaker. She'll have the black dress and the others here for the funeral." I had to chuckle at the amazement on Hilda's face. "I know," I said. "I found it hard to believe too, but she assured me it would be so. It seems Mr. Whitmore rewards handsomely when he gets his own way." I twisted the hat restlessly.

My anger was surfacing again. "He bought me dresses. He's burying my own father. I'm sure he expects me to be grateful." I sighed. "He's been very thoughtful. Too thoughtful. I'm uneasy." Another thought drove away my anger. "Do you think he'll be at the funeral? It would be very brazen of him." I pursed my lips. "I don't want him to come. If he approaches me, I'm liable to say something dreadful that both he and I might regret."

Hilda laid a soothing hand on my arm. "Don't borrow trouble, dear. Tomorrow at the funeral I'm sure he won't speak other than to express his sympathy. He's been kind. Even you've admitted that. He won't want to interfere in your grief. When he feels the time is right, he'll make the first step. Until then you'll just have to wait." She took the hat out of my hands. "I have to finish these before tomorrow. Why don't you go upstairs and have some lunch. I made a pot of stew. Fresh biscuits are in the oven. When you've eaten, lay down and rest. Tomorrow will come soon enough."

Upstairs I filled a plate then sat staring at it. My thoughts were on Grant Whitmore. I didn't think of his looks or his arrogant manner this time. I'd been trying to keep another worry at bay these last few hours, but now that I was tired and my defenses low, the thought crept out of hiding.

If I married Grant Whitmore, just how much of a wife was he expecting me to be? My cheeks flushed. I thought of him touching me. Stoutly I squared my shoulders. I wasn't going to crawl into bed with a stranger. Just because his title might be "husband" didn't change any of my feelings toward him.

I was old enough to know what happened between a man and a woman. I was also innocent enough to believe there should be love between two people before nature took over. Since I didn't love anyone, I felt sure I'd be safe. I might remain safe from Whitmore, but would I remain safe from my own needs? Unbidden, his blue eyes came to mind. Uneasily I pushed the thought away.

The morning of the funeral dawned black and dismal. Lightning flashed and the thunder rolled in the distance. Rain poured out of a leaden sky, soaking anything and everything.

Hilda and I dressed early, then watched the rain streaming down the windows. The streets were filled with buggies, as usual. Even a cold spring rain didn't deter them from coming out.

Promptly at one-thirty a black carriage pulled by matching black horses rounded the corner. I sighed shakily. "I see them coming, Hilda. Are you ready?"

Hilda adjusted her veil, then helped me arrange the folds of tulle around my own shoulders. The undertaker had an umbrella waiting for us as we stepped out into the rain. Holding it over our heads, he assisted us into the carriage.

The service passed in a blur. Before I knew it, we were being driven to Willowcrest to the family cemetery. The reverend had given Papa a fine eulogy. All his praise had made me proud. What had saddened me was the lack of attendance. I blamed the foul weather, not the indifference of Papa's old friends. There hadn't been any sign of Grant Whitmore. I ignored a brief flash of disappointment. I was curious to see him again, only with a closer inspection. I was nervous. I told myself, it was this waiting. I didn't like the idea of my future being held in another man's hands.

Up ahead the hearse carried Papa's body through the gates of Willowcrest. He'd come home at last. Tears ran down my cheeks. All through the funeral ceremony, I'd kept my tears in check, but now I cried. He was home. Home, where he belonged. There wasn't anyone or anything to take him away again. I wiped my tears away. I wouldn't cry any longer. Papa was where he wanted to be. He was at his beloved wife's side and he was on Crestwood land.

The family cemetery sat on a bluff, overlooking the dark muddy Mississippi. Willow trees grew close to the overhang, spilling their feathery branches out into the open air. A gray stone wall enclosed the area, ensuring privacy. Inside the wall all was peaceful and serene. These burial grounds had never seemed evil or frightening to me. On summer days Papa and I had brought picnic lunches and spent the day cleaning the graves of weeds. Even today I couldn't feel repulsed. The open hole where Papa was to rest didn't look ominous.

While the reverend said a word over the grave, I studied the headstone. I remembered the day it had been delivered. Papa had wanted something very special for Mama. The stone had been crated and shipped upriver from New Orleans.

Made of rose pink marble, it was carved in the shape of two entwining hearts. Around the edges of the hearts willow leaves had been deeply etched. The huge hearts rested on a block of marble. ELEANOR CRESTWOOD and the date of her birth and death had been inscribed on one heart. Until now the other heart had simply read, WILLIAM CRESTWOOD. Now the date, MARCH 24, 1845, had been added.

The reverend brought his prayer to a close. I shook hands with a few of the brave souls who had risked a soaking to stand with me at the graveside. This courtesy done, everyone hurried to their carriages. I was free to go to mine. But I remained standing.

I gazed down the bluff, absorbing the sight of my beloved home. I hadn't realized how hungry I was for a chance to see it. I stared until the undertaker tapped me on the arm. With a sigh, I stepped back into the black carriage.

That evening as Hilda and I sat around the fire, trying to drive the damp chilliness from our bones, I began to outline my plans.

"I can't sit around waiting for him to make the first move. I have to do something. If I go out to Willowcrest and face him, we can come to some sort of understanding." I paced the floor nervously. "It might be better if we meet at Willowcrest instead of here. I have enough money to hire a carriage to take me."

Hilda frowned. "I don't know if that's the right thing to do, Althea. Didn't your father say Mr. Whitmore would come for you when the time was right?"

"Yes," I agreed reluctantly. "But why should he decide the time is right? Let's look at this another way, Hilda. What if he's not as happy as Papa thought with this arrangement? What's to keep him from putting off bringing me out there?" I held out my hands. "Don't you see? Every morning I'd wake up wondering if this would be the day. I have to get it over with."

"I can understand what you're saying, but I can't stop worrying. I know you, Althea. I know your sharp tongue. I wish I could talk you out of this but . . ." Her voice trailed off as she noticed the firm set of my jaw.

My mind was made up. "I'll pack tonight. I'll leave tomorrow."

"Tomorrow?" She gaped. "So soon? Althea, I think you'd better wait a few more days."

"I can't. I'm too restless." I turned to her and spoke earnestly. "It's like a giant black cloud hanging over me. I have to make an effort to get out from under it."

Before Hilda had a chance to say anything, a heavy pounding sounded on the store door.

"Who could that be," muttered Hilda.

She started to the staircase, but I grabbed her arm. In a whisper I said, "What if it's Mr. Whitmore? What if he's come for me already?"

"Then everything would get resolved even quicker," she said.

"Yes, but he'd be in control of the situation, as before. I want the element of surprise on my side, at out first meeting. That won't happen if he's downstairs." I paced the floor quickly, jumping timidly as the pounding sounded again. "Tell him I've gone for a walk," I said haphazardly.

Hilda laughed and gestured at the rain-splattered windows. "In the rain? We both know he isn't a fool."

She didn't wait for any more of my ideas but went to the door. The hammering stopped and the murmur of voices could be heard. I strained my ears but couldn't make out a word. Hilda was back quickly, carrying a large box.

I helped her with it, placing it near the stove. As I laid it down, I noticed the name of the dressmaker I'd visited stamped across the top. "That's odd," I murmured. "All my dresses arrived first thing this morning."

Hilda added, "I hung them behind the door in your room. Did you order something else?"

I shook my head. "No. Maybe there's a note inside."

I got a sharp knife and cut through the twine. Carefully I lifted off the lid. I pushed the white tissue aside then stared into the box with horror.

Hilda drew in her breath. I turned to her and spoke through clenched teeth. "You touch it. I don't want anything to do with it."

She reached past me and took hold of the white dress by its shoulder seams. She gave it a gentle shake and watched the seed pearls, sewn to the bodice, cast a soft glow. It was a wedding dress, complete with train and veil. I could only stare at it, trembling with rage.

"How dare he!" I spluttered, stalking around the room. "How dare he!"

"Just a minute," said Hilda. "There's more."

I whirled around to watch her pull out shoes made of the finest kid leather. She laid them to one side to take out the most obscene undergarments I've ever seen. They were virginal white and covered with filmy frothy lace.

My face felt hot to the touch. I knew I was blushing scarlet. "Put those things down!" I shouted to her. "Grant Whitmore is a disgusting man. He doesn't have the right to buy these things for me." I heard the rising note of hysteria in my voice. I swallowed hard. "How dare the man!" I whispered again.

"Don't take on so, my dear. It isn't like he went in and picked them out himself. I'm sure he left instructions for the dressmaker. All he did was tell her to make up a complete ensemble. I'm sure he never set eyes on these garments, my dear."

I let my stiff shoulders go limp, relaxing the tension that gripped me. I even tried to smile. "I'm sorry, Hilda. I let my nerves carry me away. I know he didn't personally pick them out."

"You're just tired. Why don't you go to bed and sleep." Hilda quickly folded everything and put them back in the box, out of my sight. "Are your plans for tomorrow still the same?"

"Yes," I snapped, then softened my tone. "Yes, Hilda. More than ever, I have to meet him. I can't let another night go by not knowing what is going to happen. In the morning I'll leave for Willowcrest."

My voice sounded strong and sure. I acted as if I knew what I was doing. Inside I was quaking with fear. Hilda had just a small sampling as to how those wedding garments had upset me. Those light and airy feminine garments had hinted at an intimacy that wasn't to be. It seemed to bring home to me just what marriage might entail. Things had to be set straight.

Once in bed, I willed myself to sleep. It wouldn't do to appear before the royal prince with circles under my eyes. I needed a good sleep, but I didn't think it would come. It must have been the rain drumming gently on the roof that lulled me into a deep, dreamless sleep.

CHAPTER THREE

The next morning I left St. Louis in great anticipation and not without a small amount of apprehension. I didn't know how my bold action would be received.

At least the weather was on my side. I would be arriving with a warm sun at my back. All the black storm clouds of yesterday were a thing of the past. As I rode along, I took time to appreciate the fresh bright green of spring. Small wildflowers bloomed along the side of the road. This road to Willowcrest was smooth and well traveled. It ran parallel to the river, dipping away from it, then abruptly coming back again. It amazed me how I had hungered for the sight and smell of all this.

I loved it. I loved my home. Papa had instilled a deep devotion in me. As I looked out the window, I found my thoughts had helped me pass away the ride. I was looking at Crestwood land.

My heart began to beat rapidly. My hands were perspiring. I wiped them on the scrap of linen I clutched in my hand. I was nervous. How was I to handle this? Would Grant be at home? Would he consent to seeing me?

I would know soon. We had turned into the driveway and were making our way slowly to the house. I could barely contain my eagerness as I paid the arranged fee and as an afterthought added a generous tip.

Now I stood on the front steps, bag and baggage at my feet. I wondered how many eyes were staring at me from behind the curtains. It was this thought that put some stiffening in my backbone. I lifted my proud chin up a notch. Under my breath I muttered, "There's nothing to accomplish standing here."

With a false courage, I grasped the door knocker in my hand and tapped it firmly. The door began to open immediately, confirming my suspicions that my arrival had been watched. My heart leaped to my throat, then settled in its rightful place as I saw it was only John, the butler. He was getting on in years, but he'd been a kind and faithful servant to my family.

"Hello, John," I said. "It's good to see you again." I'd seen him yesterday at the funeral, so I added, "Thank you for coming to Papa's funeral. It would have pleased him to have you there."

His old face glowed with pleasure. "Miss Althea. I saw someone getting out of a buggy, but I didn't recognize it was you. Won't you come in?"

I smiled with relief. So I was to be admitted. "I'd like to see Mr. Whitmore, John. Is he in?" I looked past the old man, hoping to catch a glimpse of the new lord and master.

The entrance hall extended from front to back. Two large staircases rose from the ground floor to the second. The stairs curved up like a suspended horseshoe up to a balcony that ran the distance of three sides on the upper story.

My glance swept the hallway, loving the sight of it but disappointed to find John and me alone. "Will you let him know I'm here?" I repeated.

"Yes, Miss Althea. He's in the study." John hesitated and seemed embarrassed as he added, "Will you wait here?"

I smiled to let him know I took no offense at his remark. His position was uncomfortable. He had a new employer now, yet it would be hard to treat me as a casual visitor. He had watched me grow up. "I'll wait here, John."

With a smile of relief, he went back through the house. The view of the study door was blocked by the staircase. So I turned my attention elsewhere. All the doors off the entrance hall were closed. I wanted to check each room to see if any changes had been made but didn't want to be caught snooping. Instead, I stood quietly like the polite visitor I was.

John came back with instructions to show me to the study. I followed him, my step brisk and my manner businesslike. I swept into the study with as much grandeur as my simple gray dress and run-over black shoes would allow.

He sat at Papa's desk. Papers were scattered across its smooth top. He didn't bother to look up at my entrance but continued to read the letter in his hand. If he was trying to put me in my place, he was succeeding. I felt like a naughty child awaiting punishment.

Given the opportunity, I studied him. Grant Whitmore was even handsomer than I'd remembered. His hair was very black and curled crisply around the nape of his neck. He wore a white linen shirt that was unbuttoned to the waist, leaving his brown chest bare. I couldn't understand why the sight of his naked torso left me a bit breathless. The dark network of hairs that crisscrossed his broad chest held a deep fascination for me. It took an effort to tear my gaze away.

I lifted my eyes to his face and felt my cheeks redden with confusion. He had finished reading. Our eyes locked. I had remembered them correctly. They were a bright startling blue against the tan of his face. They stared at me unblinkingly.

I cleared my throat and shuffled my feet nervously. I waited for him to break the silence. When he didn't speak, I searched my mind for an opening remark. I had planned to control our first meeting. Instead I stood speechless. I didn't know what to say. It didn't help to have him sitting at Papa's desk, a look of irritation stamped on his features.

He rested his elbows on the desk, pressing his fingers together to form a pyramid. Over their tips, he stared at me. There was a mocking gleam in his eyes as he looked me over, from head to hoof, much as my father used to do to a new heifer.

In a deep voice, he said, "I don't remember telling you it was time to come here. Are you that anxious to wed?"

I continued to gape at him, his remark catching me unaware. I didn't grasp its meaning right away. Then his cruel words sank in. I drew a sharp breath. Fiery words fairly scorched the air between us.

"How dare you say such a thing! Up until now you've done all the directing and arranging. I didn't want to wait for your royal summons. You and Papa have an agreement. But it involves my life. I have some say in what happens." I spluttered on about my "rights" and my "future" until I ran out of words. It didn't matter. I'd lost his attention. He'd gone back to the papers on the desk.

"Well?" I snapped.

He glanced up at me. "Well what?" he countered.

I hated him for making me feel so inadequate. Now that I was face to face with the man who had caused Papa and me so much worry and sorrow, I couldn't think of a thing to say. A few days ago, words had blistered my tongue. Here he was right in front of me and I felt confused. It was this strange uncertainty that made me strike out at him for not giving me a rather unimportant courtesy.

For lack of anything better to say, I smirked, "We have things to discuss. I don't plan to do it while standing on my feet. I'll excuse your terrible manners for not coming up from your chair when I came in the room, but you could offer me a seat."

Instinctively I took a step back as Grant struggled to his feet. My chance remark had infuriated him. His eyes had lost their mocking gleam. A pinched look showed around his nose and mouth. Blue steely eyes held me motionless. Never had I seen such anger in another person's eyes, especially directed at me.

I understood and felt ashamed of my words as I watched this

tall and handsome man move with some difficulty from behind his desk. He used both hands to keep his balance. I looked down at his feet and saw the reason. One of his shoes had been specially constructed to add an inch to his game leg. Grant Whitmore was lame. What's more, he was in extreme pain. His face was blanched of its healthy tan.

I whispered, "I'm so sorry. I didn't know you were . . ." I stopped, but the damage had been done.

His eyes glared into mine. Lips barely moved as he said hoarsely, "Can't you say the word? Crippled!" His voice rose to a shout. "Get out of here, you fool! Get out of my sight!"

His voice was a roar in my ears. I stood where I was. He swung his arm around to point to the door and lost his balance. Only his quick action, grabbing the desk, saved him from falling to the floor, thus humiliating himself further. I started to go to him, but he waved me away. There was pain written plainly on his face. He closed his eyes and breathed deeply. My heart went out to him. I wanted to help him. To offer him my sympathy.

My eyes softened with pity for this proud and handsome man. It seemed only natural to ask, "How did it happen?"

His eyes quickly opened at the sound of my voice. I could see he was surprised to see me still there. Using supreme willpower, Grant pulled himself into an erect position. Holding the desk for support, he looked into my eyes. What he saw brought his fury back threefold. Through clenched teeth, he snarled, "That's none of your business. Get out of this room and take your pity with you as well! Get out! Now!" He took a deep breath and bellowed, "Raymond! Raymond, where the hell are you?"

A big burly man stepped into the room. In a glance, he sized up the situation. Quietly he said, "Please leave us, ma'am."

With one last look at Grant, I turned and ran from the room. John was waiting for me outside. One look at his face told me that he and everyone else in the house had heard Grant's words. I tried to smile, but it was a feeble effort.

"I'm afraid I haven't made a very good impression, John. Mr Whitmore told me to get out. Am I to leave the house or just his sight?"

"I'm sure he meant the study, Miss Althea. He's instructed me to take your bags, if you brought any, up to your choice of rooms. I've taken them to your old room."

Tears threatened. "Thank you. I'm going for a walk in the cemetery, if anyone needs me." I laughed bitterly. "Which I'm sure won't happen."

John opened the front door for me, then stood aside for me to pass. I stopped to look up at his kind old face. "I know I shouldn't question you, but I wondered if you knew what happened. Was he in an accident?"

John's face closed like a book. He was a faithful servant. He wouldn't gossip with me, an outsider. "I'd rather not say, ma'am. He's a good man. I'd not like to upset him. When he wishes it, he'll speak to you."

Apparently my disappointment was evident, for he added in a low whisper, "He's in terrible pain, miss. He twisted his bad leg the other day getting down from his carriage. It has made him a bit testy."

"I see," I murmured. "Testy" was hardly the word I would have used to describe Grant's fury. I smiled up at John and went down the steps and out to my garden. My thoughts were confusing. I'd surprised Grant with my arrival, just as I'd planned. Seeing him had done something to me I hadn't counted on. I felt ashamed of my reaction to his bared torso. I'd stood mute. Then his words came back to me. "Anxious to wed." Was that what he thought was behind my arrival at Willowcrest? If so, he didn't know how wrong he was. Instead of setting things straight, my coming had made more problems. Harsh words and misconstrued actions would have to be explained.

I didn't look forward to my next confrontation with Mr. Grant Whitmore. I put that thought behind me and took solace in my garden. I would find a few flowers and go visit my parents' grave.

CHAPTER FOUR

My first week at Willowcrest passed without incident. I tried to avoid any more scenes with Grant. If our paths inadvertently crossed, I nodded courteously. That was it. I ate alone in the large dining room while Grant took a tray in his room.

I'd been surprised to find there were only four house servants at Willowcrest. John, Sarah, the maid, Agnes, the cook, and her son Jeremy, who did odd jobs around the house. Raymond acted as overseer. He was more a friend of Grant's than a servant.

My days were spent outside watching the new season unfold. Before my eyes, I could see things greening and trees sprouting new leaves. I was also reacquainting myself with my old home. There were few changes. My biggest surprise was the redecoration of the master bedroom. I had noticed it quite by accident one afternoon. Grant and Raymond had gone into town to see the doctor. Finding the bedroom door open, I couldn't resist peeking into Grant's private domain. I didn't enter the room but stared in open-mouthed wonder.

When Papa and Mama had shared it, it had been a somber room. Somber was hardly the word to describe it now. Light green brocade covered the walls. Darker green carpet lay upon the floor. The giant canopied bed rested on a dais two steps above the floor. It was the bed that held my attention. I wondered why this was the one room Grant had changed. Was it to brighten the room or was there another motive? I quickly moved away from the room, but thoughts of that bed came to me at odd moments of the day and night. Was it a marriage bed he had prepared? I didn't know. I wasn't sure I wanted to find out.

Marriage hadn't been mentioned and I wasn't going to force the issue. I was lulled into a false hope these days. I liked this simple arrangement. I was back at Willowcrest. Even sharing the house with Grant wasn't bothersome. We were two strangers living together but separately under the same roof.

I was curious about this bitter man. I wondered how lame he was when not hampered by his latest injury. I knew he always wore shoes or boots specially designed to compensate for his leg.

What interested me even more was how it had happened. He'd told me it wasn't any of my business and I knew he was right. Still I guessed. Had he been shot while cheating at cards? I had heard tales about the rousing parties aboard riverboats. One time I might have believed that of him, but after meeting him I wasn't as sure. It was hard to picture Grant a cheater. He looked very capable of dealing with any situation. I admitted I found his lean dark looks appealing, even exciting, but his bitterness and masterful ways provoked me.

Knowing this, I stayed out of his way. I knew my freedom had come to an end the day he searched me out. I'd started the afternoon resting on a bench in the garden. Now I was down on my hands and knees weeding a flower bed. It was his uneven steps on the stones that caught my attention. I got up quickly, an uneasiness in the pit of my stomach.

"I'd like a word with you," he said curtly.

"Of course," I murmured. I followed him to a bench, then sat quietly, my dirty hands folded tightly in my lap. I waited for him to speak. I could see he was disturbed. He didn't waste any time laying the blame on me.

"When you came out here, I knew it would bring trouble. I was right. While in town today, I heard some rumors that have to be dispelled. When William died I planned to give you a few days to adjust before coming for you." He turned to me with a frown. "You took matters into your own hands. We'll be married tomorrow."

He might as well have announced his intention to fly across the river. I couldn't have been more surprised. I began to shake my head. "No. I have no intention of marrying you tomorrow."

Grant opened his mouth, but I rushed on ahead. "This agreement was between you and Papa. I didn't know it existed until right before he died. I don't see how you can consider marrying a person you don't know. We're strangers," I said unnecessarily. Then I asked, "Why would a man like you be willing to settle for this kind of a marriage?"

"A man like me?" he repeated bitterly. Grant crossed the terrace to gaze out across the river.

I came to stand at his side but kept my eyes on him. I knew the river's colors, moods and curves by heart. What I was finding more exciting was the clash of emotions on Grant's face.

When he spoke, it was to ignore my question. He said, "Since you have a copy of the agreement, you're aware of its conditions. I'm willing for this marriage to take place. If you aren't, pack your bags. Raymond will take you back to town." On this last word, he faced me with a lazy smile, then walked away as quickly as his leg would permit.

I was furious. I knew the conditions only too well. They were burned in my mind. He was safe. I was the one in the predicament. I had to marry him or leave. That was my choice. It was time to take a stand. Once I had his name, would he expect more? He spoke of the agreement's conditions. Well, I had a few conditions of my own.

My head was held high as I marched into his study. I was ready to do battle. I cleared my throat and almost lost my nerve as he looked up from his interrupted work.

"I'd like a word with you," I said. Before he had a chance to give me one of his cutting remarks, I began. "I've come to a decision." My voice became sarcastic. "I'll accept your proposal of marriage, but I have some conditions too."

I saw the mulish look on his face, but I ignored it. "I'll be your wife in name only. I'll continue to live in my own room. You'll stay in yours." Before I'd finished speaking, Grant threw back his head, roaring with laughter.

I didn't know what to make of this side of him. I could only stare. After several minutes of this uncontrolled mirth, I put my hands on my hips. My voice was cool.

"I'm glad you think this humorous. It doesn't matter, as long as you uphold my wishes."

He stopped laughing but continued to chuckle. "I'm sorry, but I really couldn't help myself." He came around the desk to hand me something he'd taken from a drawer.

It was a small hand mirror. In its depths I saw a young woman with a dirty face and limp strands of hair hanging about her ears. The sun bonnet was crooked, the brim misshapen, tilting up at an odd angle. I waved the mirror away with an embarrassed flush.

Grant wore a smirk on his full lips. "Do you think I'll have any trouble leaving you alone? Every time I've seen you, your hair is falling down. All week you've crawled among the weeds and dirt. Your clothes have a servant's air about them." He shook his head. "Ma'am, it will be my pleasure to have separate bedrooms and separate lives. That was my plan all along." He sat back down at the desk. "Now, if you'll excuse me, I have work to do."

I couldn't leave fast enough. I was mortified. With just a few words, Grant had pronounced me unappealing and unattractive. It was a severe blow to my ego.

I ran from the room and from the house. Though I ran swiftly, my thoughts kept step with me. I was deeply hurt. It was one thing for me to say I didn't want anything from Grant but quite another to be told he had nothing to give. I should have felt safe knowing he'd leave me alone, but I felt like I'd been robbed of something that might have been worth having.

I felt alone as I stood there in the woods. I honestly asked myself if it would be enough for me to have Willowcrest and my gardening. Didn't I want more for myself? Love? Companionship? Someone to need and want me? Stubbornly I shook my head. I would make do with what I had. I'd marry Grant. I'd be polite. But that was all. I didn't need him either. I'd never let him know how deep his words had wounded me.

I walked slowly back to the house only to come face to face with Grant at the bottom of the staircase. He looked me up and down, his mouth opening and closing a couple of times. Sadly he shook his head.

He didn't need to say a word. His blue eyes had said it all. I looked terrible. My eyes were red from my tears. My bonnet had slipped down to my shoulders, leaving my hair to fly in uncontrollable abandon. I ignored him. Putting my nose in the air, I flounced past him and up the stairs to my room.

I hoped to find some solitude here, but I was wrong. It looked like someone was turning my comfortable bedroom into a dress shop. Boxes, tissue and clothes lay all over my bed and chairs. I stopped inside the door and stared at the confusion. When I could find my voice, I cried, "What in the world is all of this?"

Sarah was like a child at Christmas. Her eyes were shining happily. "Look, miss. It's a surprise from Mr. Whitmore. He brought the boxes back from town."

From where I stood, I could count seven new dresses on the

bed and five more hanging in the wardrobe. I saw underwear, petticoats, capes, shoes, lacy shawls and silk scarves. Sarah shoved a cape into my arms. It was made of emerald silk with strips of silver fox fur trim. Another done in gold and black lay across my desk. I smoothed the soft fur absently, my mind elsewhere.

My first thought was How kind of Grant. Then I recalled our recent conversation. He hadn't liked the way I looked, so he was doing me over. I tossed the cape back to the bed. Over my shoulder, I told Sarah, "You finish putting these things away. I'll be back."

I knew Grant would be in his room, dressing for dinner. I stepped quickly around the balcony to knock sharply on his door. Grant answered the door himself. He'd begun to change. Lather was spread across his cheeks. He was stripped to the waist, and I noticed how his tight pants hugged his narrow hips. As before, I was intrigued to see the way the black chest hair traveled down his chest to disappear under the band of his trousers. Once again I was conscious of a breathlessness.

I cleared my throat and with trembling hands tried to smooth my hair. I'd lost the hairpins somewhere between the house and the woods. In silence I gaped at Grant, forgetting what I'd come to his room for.

"Have you lost your waspish tongue as well as your pins? I'm sure if you look carefully in those boxes, you'll see some have been enclosed."

"Why did you buy me these things?" I whispered, keeping my eyes averted from his naked chest and the huge bed I could see over his shoulder.

"Why shouldn't I? I'm tired of your depressing black and gray. It will lift my spirits to see you in a blue or a gold." He smiled almost pleasantly as he said, "You didn't need to come over here to thank me. I'm well aware of your gratitude. Just get changed. I don't like to be kept waiting. I'm joining you for dinner tonight."

He said it like I should be thankful for his presence. I looked at his back. I had been dismissed. I wished I had the nerve to strike him, but I didn't. Instead I used my tongue to wound him.

"I'm afraid you'll have a long wait, if you expect me to join you for dinner. I'm sure you'll enjoy your dinner better without my unappealing looks seated across from you. I know I'll enjoy mine if spared the sight of you." I curtsied mockingly, then started back to my room.

"If you don't eat in the dining room, you don't eat at all," he warned. "There won't be any tray brought up to you."

I heard him. His tone was hardly muted. I chose to ignore him. I was too upset to eat. After a bath I was ready for bed. But once there, I couldn't sleep.

Our exchange of angry words rolled through my mind, along with the sobering fact that I had agreed to marry this man. Was I doing the right thing? All week I'd looked here and there for the jewels, but I hadn't begun a systematic search. I was sure Grant had hoped I'd back out of the agreement at the last minute, but I couldn't. I wouldn't let him have Willowcrest for his own. It was this thought that let me relax.

I was home. Grant wouldn't frighten me or drive me or even humiliate me from my rightful place. Papa had fixed it so I could live here. I would stay at all costs.

My dreams were troubled that night, but I awoke to find the room bright with sunshine. My wedding day. In a few short hours, I'd be Mrs. Grant Whitmore. I'd be tied for life to a man I didn't know. Furthermore, I wasn't sure I cared to find out.

Ours was a marriage of convenience. No love was involved. The only solution to my predicament might be if I found the jewels and they were tempting enough to make Grant leave. I'd be free of him. Free to marry the man I chose. I was unprepared for a sharp stab of remorse.

I looked in my mirror, searching my eyes. I tried to read what I saw. Sadness? Why? Grant meant nothing to me. All I felt for him was anger and exasperation. Those weren't emotions you could base a happy marriage on.

All too soon the clock chimed the hour of my wedding. Grant was soon to be my husband. I'd always thought weddings to be solemn and joyous occasions. Mine was only solemn. Grant and I had nothing to smile about. The only joy was in Sarah's eyes. She was a romantic and sure Grant and I had declared our undying love for each other.

I couldn't meet Grant's eyes. I was afraid of what I might see in their blue depths. I willed myself to stand straight and tall. I wouldn't let him know I was afraid and having second thoughts.

In record time, or so it seemed to me, the deed was done. Just a few words from a man I didn't know. My signature on a piece of paper and I was tied to Grant for the rest of my life. My left hand felt unusually heavy with the weight of the wide gold band on my finger. Just another reminder of my new status.

After the ceremony I would have been content to spend the rest of the day in my garden, but the servants had arranged a special brunch to be served to the happy bride and groom. So Grant and I ate our first meal together as man and wife.

I didn't have any appetite, but Grant ate with enthusiasm. I pushed the tender pink ham around my plate, trying to look as if I was delighted with this development. When I thought I'd stayed as long as necessary, I got up from the table.

Grant looked at me, one eyebrow raised questioningly.

"I've finished," I murmured in way of explanation.

"Your appetite wasn't up to par. I'd have thought going without supper last night would have left you ravenous."

"I've eaten enough." I turned to go, but his next words stopped me.

"I have a present for you."

I turned back to see him lay a leather case near my plate. He gestured to it. "Go ahead. Open it."

I did as he directed and breathed a silent "Oh."

Against a black velvet background lay a topaz necklace with matching earrings. "They're beautiful." I looked up, meeting my new husband's eyes. We stared at each other quietly, the space of the table separating us. Without thinking, I let my eyes stray to the gentle curve of his full lips. I remembered their soft fleeting kiss at the close of our vows. Not waiting to see what remark he might make, I stumbled from the room, bewildered by the tears in my eyes.

CHAPTER FIVE

I hung my wasted wedding gown far to the back of the wardrobe. For such a short time, one of my regular dresses would have been adequate. Even one of the black ones would have suited my mood. I had sat down at the window when John brought word that Grant wanted to see me. I felt my pulse quicken, wondering what he wanted. I took a moment to smooth my hair before knocking on the study's closed door.

Upon entering, I was surprised to find a smile on Grant's face. I tried to give him an answering smile, but my stiff lips refused to move. I asked, "You wished to see me?"

Grant held a chair, then waited until I was settled. "I realize," he began, "our marriage isn't an ordinary one, but the results are the same. I thought we might go to the theater tonight as a way of marking the event."

I was thrilled with his suggestion. I knew my eyes were shining with delight. "What a wonderful idea," I said.

"I thought we would start with a leisurely meal in town." He glanced at his watch and asked, "Can you be ready to leave in about an hour?"

"Yes, of course." This time I found it very easy to smile. "Thank you for including me." I hurried from the room, riding on a cloud. It had been years since I'd been to the theater. That was why I felt so elated. My feelings had nothing to do with the idea I'd be spending the entire evening in Grant's company.

Upstairs I rang for Sarah, then turned to survey my new wardrobe. I chose a taffeta gown that was the color of burnished gold and would enhance Grant's wedding gift.

The dress's neckline was more daring than I was used to. It formed a deep V above my breasts before slipping elegantly off my shoulders. Small ruffles completed the sleeves. The bodice was tight at my waist before flaring out into a three-tiered skirt. Black lace scallops showed around the bottom of each ruffled tier.

I felt very fashionable as I hooked my new necklace around my neck. In the light the topaz gleamed and glittered extravagantly. I looked back at my mirror and gasped with disappointment. I'd forgotten my heavy unwielding hair. I relied heavily on Sarah to help, and she didn't fail me. Seeing what was needed, she quickly left me only to return with a device used to curl hair.

The next half hour passed very slowly and tediously. When Sarah finally allowed me a glance in the mirror, I caught my breath in wonder. I looked like a different person. She had curled my hair in loose ringlets using my gold combs to pull it back from my face. The long auburn curls cascaded down my back. Two tendrils strayed near my ears, softening my features.

I smiled at the beaming Sarah and tried to thank her, but she brushed my praise away, telling me to hurry. She pressed a cape into my arms and opened the bedroom door.

I walked slowly down the stairs, my eyes on Grant's face, searching it for some clue as to what he thought. If I had expected a compliment from him, I was disappointed. He nodded to me and glanced at his watch. I heard him tell John to lock up and he hustled me out to the buggy. We were on our way.

We rode in silence. I searched my mind for a safe topic but could think of none save the weather. Since this was too mundane, I remained quiet, basking in the late afternoon sun. I was content to watch Grant's strong expert hands on the reins. I didn't even try to understand why they gave me a thrill.

Grant chose the Grand Hotel for our dining. I was impressed with the number of well-dressed people who knew him. Some merely nodded, while others called Grant by name. I wondered if they were old gambling friends. Then I felt ashamed of myself for such a snide thought.

Grant was being nice to me, though his manner was a trifle stiff. I couldn't quite put my finger on what was bothering me. He smiled politely. He saw to it that my wineglass was filled and the meal was to my satisfaction. Yet it was as if he held himself in reserve. As if he didn't want to get too close. Too involved. This was puzzling. Why should he worry? He'd made his feelings very clear.

I tried to forget about him. As I looked around the crowded room, my attention was caught by a group of people across the way. It wasn't the people at the table but one of the men. As our eyes met, he grinned most beguilingly. I almost returned his smile but caught myself in time. I quickly looked away, taking a drink of wine. I could feel his eyes on me. After a moment or two, I let my eyes travel around the room. Once again I encountered him. He had been sitting there waiting for me to look his way. This time his eyes stared deep into mine before looking at his companion, then back to me. I blushed. He seemed to be saying he wished I were his dinner partner. I was embarrassed by his boldness. I pulled my chair up closer to our table so I might avoid him.

If Grant noticed my discomfort, he ignored it. Then to my

chagrin Grant saw someone he wanted to speak to. After assuring me he would be right back, he walked from the dining room.

I sipped my drink, keeping my eyes glued to the tabletop. I didn't want to encourage the man across the room. I should have known from his earlier behavior he didn't need encouragement. Grant had only stepped through the door when I felt the stranger at my elbow. For a time, I pretended he wasn't there, but I wasn't that good an actress. Coolly I looked up, meeting his laughing gray eyes.

"Yes," I said crisply. "May I help you?"

He bowed formally and sighed, his hand above his heart. "Say you'll have dinner with me one night next week and I'll die a happy man."

I didn't know what to say. I'd never been talked to or looked at in this manner. I felt my fair skin redden under his open admiring gaze. His eyes traveled over my bare arms to rest lightly on the necklace.

"Your jewels fail to compete with the soft glow of your eyes, my dear. May I inquire your name?"

I opened my mouth, but it was Grant's deep voice I heard. He had come unnoticed to the table.

"This is my wife, sir." He spoke sharply. "Who are you and what do you want?"

The man straightened slowly before turning to Grant. He seemed surprised. "You don't know me?" he asked.

"Should I?" muttered Grant.

"You don't remember me at all?" repeated the man.

"I said I didn't." Grant didn't bother to hide his irritation.

The interloper grinned broadly. He clapped Grant on the shoulder. "Don't get mad. I just found it hard to believe you didn't know me. After all, I remember you very well." He bowed to Grant and said, "My name is Thomas Campbell. I suppose you don't recognize the name. We weren't properly introduced. We met about a year ago on board ship. You cleaned me out." He turned to me. "Your husband has a very good poker face. He beat me with two eights. I was sure he was holding a full house." The man spoke in a laughing manner, but there was a serious note underneath. "I'd like a rematch, Mr. Whitmore. Everyone needs a chance to recoup his losses."

Grant didn't hesitate. He shook his head. "I'm sorry, but I don't gamble anymore. I've given it up. If I were to play again, it would be in the parlor of my own home with some old friends. The highest stake would be for a bottle of port. Nothing more."

Grant dismissed Campbell as he turned to help me from my chair. It was I who saw the venomous glare flung at Grant's unguarded back. Only I saw the thinly veiled hostility toward my husband. Before I could blink, the look was gone. Campbell smiled suavely at me, lowering one eyelid in a lewd wink.

I was shaken by his hatred for Grant and repulsed by his unabashed flirting with me. I didn't trust this man. I knew if he got the chance he'd do me or Grant harm. I hurried away from the table as fast as I could without drawing attention to my fear.

Campbell stayed on my mind all the way to the theater, but once inside, I forgot everything but the evening ahead of me. I was thrilled to see Grant had taken a box for the season. Perhaps this was just the first of many such outings together.

The play was a lighthearted comedy, which suited my taste for the evening. I didn't feel able to cope with someone else's troubles, even if fictitious.

Reality came back all too quickly as the curtain came down for intermission. Grant went to get us a refreshing drink. I was lost in thought when I felt a hand touch me lightly on the shoulder. I turned with a smile, sure it was Grant back with my drink. Instead I looked up into Campbell's eyes.

I would have gotten to my feet, but the pressure of his hand increased. I couldn't get up without creating a scene. I sat still and put a smile on my lips. But my words held no welcome for this man.

"What are you doing here?" I hissed.

"At last we're alone, my pet. I thought that dragon of a husband would never leave." He leaned forward.

I moved back as far as I could and glanced around the theater. All I needed was for Grant to hear some unfounded gossip about his new wife. I willed myself to stay calm. In a low undertone I said, "Get your bloody hands off me! My husband will be back soon. I don't want him to find you here."

"So my sweet little kitten has claws. Good! I like my women to have spunk." He took his hand away only to try to capture my hand. I quickly hid it in a fold of my skirt. He admitted defeat graciously.

"Very well." He smiled. "I'll leave as you have requested, but I'll carry the memory of your lovely face in my heart forever."

His words sickened me. I could only pray they hadn't been overheard. His praise had rung phony to me. What was his game? Why all this ridiculous declaring of admiration for me?

As for the rest of the play, he had ruined it for me. I couldn't keep my mind on it. I was worried. I wondered if I should warn Grant. Then I asked myself, Warn him about what? All I had seen was a look in the dining room of the Grand Hotel. Even then it happened so fast I wasn't sure that I'd seen it. If I told Grant what I felt, he'd think me even more of a fool than he already did.

I pondered whether or not to say anything all the way home. By the time we'd pulled into the driveway, I'd made up my mind to remain silent. I was so sleepy I could hardly keep my eyes open. As Grant helped me down from the buggy, I murmured something about a nice evening.

"You go on in. I'll see about the horses."

I only nodded. I was tired, but I'd also heard that odd note in his voice. He might have been addressing a total stranger, so impersonal was his tone. I had hoped our evening out would have helped bridge that gap between us, but apparently it hadn't.

My wedding day. My wedding night. I laughed bitterly as I crawled into my empty bed.

CHAPTER SIX

The next two weeks passed slowly. We adjusted easily to a simple routine. Grant and I ate dinner together, but the rest of the day was spent as we chose.

Grant was busy getting a herd of steers ready for slaughter. This was his first big sale since becoming the new owner of Willowcrest. He hired extra men but wanted to oversee the entire project himself.

I used Grant's time away from the house to search for the jewels. Telling Agnes and Sarah it was time to give the house a good cleaning gave me the excuse I needed to look in every nook and cranny. All week we had mopped floors, beaten rugs, wiped down woodwork and washed windows. All I'd gotten for my trouble was rough red hands and a sore back.

At night I lay in bed remembering Papa's last words. "A place where we've found much pleasure." I felt sure the jewels weren't hidden in the house. That left the out-of-doors, a thought that was staggering. I remembered all the trails we'd ridden over. All the different places we had walked and talked by. There wasn't any one place that stood out in my mind.

To get my mind off my troubles, I decided to spend the day in the garden. Grant was in the study. That was another reason to be out doors. I wanted to stay as far from him as possible. He was in a horrible mood. Yesterday while out riding, he'd hurt his bad leg. All morning he had been snapping and growling at John and Raymond and anyone else who came in contact with him.

I was enjoying myself out in the garden. It was so quiet and peaceful until I heard Grant's roar. I knew something entirely different had happened. This wasn't his roar of pain. Someone or something had angered him. I prayed it hadn't been me.

I got to my feet and hurried to the study. Raymond followed me in. We stopped inside the door. Grant was at his desk, but at our entrance he limped toward us. I didn't like the look on his face and would have stepped back, but Raymond's bulk was in the way. So I cringed as Grant towered over me.

"Of all the fool ideas. Blast his stupid meddling old hide!"

I ducked as he raised his hand, but it was only to fling a piece of paper at me. I glanced at it, then back at Grant, wondering if I was to read it. He nodded curtly.

I walked to the window and read the short note aloud. I watched for a reason why it should provoke such a response from my husband.

Dearest Grant,

Your father isn't well. Since you won't come to him, he's coming to you. We will arrive on the twentieth of April. Hope to find you and your new wife well and happy. There will be three of us. My love to you.

Aunt Celia

"I'm sorry about your father," I murmured. "Today is the fourteenth. We have less than a week to get ready."

"I can count," he snarled at me. He turned to Raymond. "What am I to do? I don't want them here. If I see that old man again . . . All we do is fight and argue."

In my own blundering way, I tried to reassure my husband.

"I think this is nice. I'm happy to get the chance to meet your family. They won't be any trouble. It might be fun to have some guests. Of course Agnes and Sarah will have to have some extra help."

Grant stood clenching and unclenching his fists. In a low voice, he explained, "You don't understand. I've told them we're happily married. I never told them of our agreement." He gave a short bark of laughter. "How will it look to them? We barely speak to each other. After only two weeks of marital bliss, we sleep in separate bedrooms." He whirled around, running his fingers through his thick hair. "This is the worst mess I've ever been in."

It didn't seem like such a terrible problem. I shrugged in a matter-of-fact way. "I don't see any reason to be so upset. Your mother and father must be as old as Papa was. They shouldn't be too hard to fool. For the short time they're here, we'll just have to pretend we're happy. As for sleeping arrangements," I paused, feeling his mocking blue eyes on my face. "I'll go into your room at night. After everyone has settled down, I'll return to my own room. I'm sure it will all work out fine."

Grant closed his eyes, moaning as if in great pain. I wondered if his leg had begun to throb again. He soon let me know what was paining him. He shook his head in disbelief while staring in amazement at Raymond.

"Did you hear her? Father may be an old goat, but he isn't senile." Grant raised his voice and thudded his fist on the desk. "Neither is my aunt. She'd see through it all in a minute." He took a deep breath and tried to control his temper. "As for my mother, she's dead. Has been for nearly twenty years." His voice choked up, but he muttered, "Father has remarried. Helene will be the hardest one to fool of them all."

I didn't know what to say. I'd been put in my place. My idea was all but crammed down my throat. I folded my arms in exasperation. He didn't like what I thought we could do, so let him think of his own plan. I held up my chin. "I've told you what I think," I said.

No one paid any attention. Grant sat at his desk, his dark angry eyes fixed out into space. I thought of leaving the study but was curious to know why Grant was so upset. He had repeated himself enough about his feud with his father, but somehow it all wasn't enough. I wondered what else was behind his anxiousness concerning the arrival of his family.

It was Grant leaving his desk that brought my attention back to him. I met his eyes and caught my breath at the bright light that shone out at me. I looked away but felt compelled to meet his glance again. I saw his mouth curve into a soft smile.

With apprehension, I watched him approach me. I stood still as he gently put his arms around my waist. Tenderly, like I was a fragile piece of china, he pulled me up against his chest. He tilted up my chin so our eyes locked. I was thrilled by his touch. His eyes seemed to hypnotize me, making it impossible to move.

His kiss began gently but increased in pressure and passion. It sent my senses reeling. I was really enjoying it when his arms dropped away. The smooth warm lips left mine. I opened my eyes dreamily to find I was alone. Grant had gone to Raymond. A big smile of success spread across his face.

"Well?" he said rubbing his hands together. "What do you think? Was it good enough to fool them?"

Grant ignored my sharp exclamation of amazement. He continued, "It'll be even better when Althea does her part." He turned back to me with a hearty smile. "I liked your idea. Those actors at the theater can't begin to compete with us, Althea."

"My idea?" I murmured. I didn't have this in mind when I said we could pretend to be happy. I was hurt and humiliated. My voice was low but deadly. "That was a mean thing to do. I loathe you and if you think I'll help you, you're mistaken. I could care less what your family thinks of our marriage and of me." Without thinking, I took a quick swipe at his face. I connected with a loud smack.

The sound of it echoing around the room surprised me almost as much as it did Grant. Before he had time to recover, I whirled out of the room, banging the front door behind me.

I went to the cemetery. I'd always found peace there. I needed answers. For those I would have to look deep inside myself. I'd admitted to an attraction for Grant right from the start. I'd forgotten my resentment toward him when I found out there had been no game of cards and that he had not taken advantage of Papa.

Since coming to Willowcrest, I'd told myself the rapid acceleration of my heart when Grant came near was due to my fear of another shouting match. I knew the truth after tasting the tender passion of his kiss. I wanted confrontations. I yearned for them. The feel of his lips, the comfort and security of his strong arms were things I'd never experienced before. I wanted to feel them around me again but not as part of an act.

I accepted the truth. I wanted Grant to love me. I wanted him to desire me. My sobs quieted. I straightened up to look around me. I'd been forced to face my feelings squarely. Now I had to decide how to deal with them. Above all, Grant must not find out how I feel. I could deal with his anger, even his arrogant manner, but never his rejection.

I let myself dream. Could I make him look at me differently? Why couldn't he fall in love with me? Thanks to him I now had beautiful clothes. Sarah had shown me how to wear my hair so it wasn't nearly as wild. What if I went along with his plan but carried it further? I would flirt with him. Lead him on. I thought of the fire in his eyes and wondered if I was getting in over my head. Being coquettish was something I'd never done. I was too open and outspoken to resort to childish games. And yet what I planned was anything but childish.

I walked slowly back to the house. My anger had cooled. I decided that if Grant asked me again to play his game, I would agree. It was with some surprise that I found him waiting for me in my bedroom. I quickly concealed my nervousness at having him so close after admitting my feelings.

"What do you want?" I demanded.

"My dear, why should you question my presence in your bedroom? We're married. Or have you forgotten?"

My eyes narrowed suspiciously. "No, I haven't forgotten, but apparently my slap knocked the conditions of our marriage out of your head. Or have you decided to violate those as well?"

A muscle jerked spasmodically in his clenched jaw, but he held his temper. "I don't hold with striking a woman. However, if you'd stayed a moment longer, I might have made an exception with you. I'll be willing to forgive you, if you'll help me with my plan."

"How kind of you," I mocked. "And am I to forgive *you?*"

"For what?" he said with raised eyebrows, "a simple kiss? I'm very sure you've been kissed before."

I turned so he couldn't see the truth in my eyes. It had been my first kiss. It took an effort, but my voice was impersonal. "Why is it so important for your family to think we're happily married?"

He started to say it wasn't any of my business but stopped. "It all happened a long time ago. None of it concerns you."

I went to the washbasin and poured water into the bowl, pretending to be unconcerned. I bathed my face and washed my hands. As I hung up the towel, I turned to find Grant watching me. I could see he was irritated but was holding his temper, not wanting to provoke me. This thought made me grin at him. That did it.

"Are you going to do it or not?" he blustered.

"I'm not sure," I said, toying with him. "I don't suppose it will hurt anyone."

"Of course it won't," he agreed, pressing his advantage. "In fact, it would make Father happy to know I'm settled. Aunt Celia would be pleased too."

"And your stepmother?" I asked.

Grant's face was blank. He finally shrugged and nodded his head.

"Well," I murmured. "All right. I'll do it, but I have to know something about you and your background."

He started to shake his head no, but I overrode his objection. "If I'm supposed to be in love with you, don't you think I should know a few personal facts. Before today I didn't know your real mother was dead. Don't you think that might strike your family as odd?"

He agreed reluctantly. "What do you want to know?"

"Little things," I said. "I don't know when your birthday is or how old you are. If I answer a simple question wrong, the whole plan would fall apart."

"I'm thirty years old and was born on October fifteenth." He stomped about the room, his voice full of exasperation. "This is stupid. My family won't be questioning you about me. They know me. What they'll be interested in is our life here at Willowcrest. I think the simple truth will be best, up to a point. The agreement won't be mentioned. We'll tell them it was your father's wish we marry."

"Do you have any brothers or sisters?"

"I had a brother, Nick. He died about three years ago."

"I'm sorry. Was he older or younger than you?" I asked.

"He was two years younger."

"How did he die?"

Grant looked pained by my questions, but he answered. "His horse bolted."

"Were you and he close?"

"He was a good brother. I was away from home when he was growing up." Grief for his dead brother was in evidence. He cleared his throat and said, "If you have no more questions . . ."

But I did. I dreaded saying the words, but I had to know. "How did you hurt your leg?"

For a minute I thought he was going on out the door, but he didn't. He almost smiled at me. "It wasn't any mysterious accident, Althea. I did a foolish thing. I jumped my horse over a fence when the ground was too wet. He missed his footing. I fell off and broke my leg. It didn't mend right, leaving one leg shorter than the other."

His voice became scornful. "I believe the correct word is 'crippled.' " He raised his eyebrows. "You've never said how you feel about being married to a man who's lame. Or you could say, 'maimed,' 'deformed,' 'disabled.' " He snorted, "I've heard them all."

"Stop it!" I said. "You aren't any of those things. When your leg is healed from this recent accident, your limp will hardly be noticeable."

He only looked at me with a scowl of distrust and of doubt. I returned his look, but mine was searching, trying to see past his bitterness. Softly I said, "Why do you say these things? Who hurt you? Who made you so bitter?"

Grant swung away from me to stalk to the door. He ignored my questions. "Is there anything else you want to know?" he said, but the impersonal note was back in his voice. His mask of bitterness had slipped for a brief moment. I had caught a glimpse of the man inside. Grant had been hurt one time or maybe more than once. It was a part of his protective armor to strike out first before he was hit.

I went along with him. I asked, "What is your father like? Will he be kind to me?"

Grant forgot his own problems as he threw back his head to laugh. "Arthur Whitmore is a bully and an outspoken old man. He does what suits him, regardless of the feelings of others. As for how he'll treat you, that remains to be seen."

"And your Aunt Celia? Is she your mother's or father's sister?"

"She's father's, but all she shares with him is the last name, 'Whitmore.' She's as kind and understanding as the old man is difficult. She lives at Whitmore Halls. Has all of her life. She's an old maid."

Before I could ask another question, Grant said, "This is it. Any more questions you have will have to—"

"Helene." I said the word softly and it hung on the air between us. I watched Grant's jaw tighten.

"What about her," he said.

"What's she like?"

"What is Helene like?" he repeated. "You'll have to see for yourself. She and my father were married after I left the Halls." He paused for a second, then said, "She was my brother's widow."

He waited for my look of surprise and grinned in satisfaction. I had a question on the tip of my tongue, but he forestalled me. "I was sure that would catch your attention. I know nothing of the circumstances of their marriage. I don't care to know. Soon you can see my esteemed family for yourself."

Grant opened the door and stepped out into the hall. "I have work to do, if you'll excuse me."

"I have some more questions, but they can wait," I said as I followed him to the door.

He grinned down at me and leaned back in the open doorway. In a low voice he asked, "Would you like a dress rehearsal this evening? I can make sure we aren't disturbed. We will perfect our act."

I gave him the only answer I could. I slammed the door in his face, then listened in irritation to him laughing at me and my confusion.

CHAPTER SEVEN

With company coming, I had little time to look for the jewels. Guests meant the hiring and training of extra servants. I also had to move all my belongings into the master bedroom. I had fought this part of Grant's plan but couldn't come up with one excuse that didn't sound childish. Grant's blue eyes, taunting and daring me, were my undoing. I wasn't a prude, I assured him, and just because I was going along with this move didn't mean a rejection of my marriage conditions. Grant had listened to my stiff old-maidish words, then had turned and gone whistling off to his study. I was left feeling very uneasy about the coming week.

As it turned out, I wasn't the only one. As the hour approached for their arrival, I sensed a turmoil in Grant. He'd spoken often enough of the friction between him and his father, but what I saw in his nervousness stemmed from a different cause. I was worried about this charade of ours. But most of all it was that huge bed upstairs. It intimidated me and tonight I would be sharing it with Grant.

I paced the hall, my eyes on the clock. It helped when Grant joined me. Some of what I was feeling must have shown on my face. He grinned and said, "Relax. They aren't savages. They don't bite." His smile deepened as he added, "At least not enough to draw blood. Father's been known to nip once or twice."

I sighed and gestured toward the study. "Would you like a glass of port before they get here?"

"As you wish. Shall I pour you one?"

I started to shake my head no, then changed my mind. I might need a little extra courage to get me through the next hours. "Please," I said.

Grant poured us each a stout drink. I watched him raise his glass in a toast, then down it quick and neat. I followed his lead, tipping up my glass.

When the fiery liquor touched my throat, I gasped for air. Tears blinded me and my stomach felt like I'd swallowed a red-hot coal. I choked and spluttered, "My God." I coughed. "How do you stand this horrible stuff?"

Grant laughed heartily. "Althea, you shouldn't have drunk it so quickly. I thought you knew to sip it. It's an acquired taste."

I used my handkerchief to wipe my teary eyes. "I feel very silly . . ." I began, but wheels in the front driveway drove my words from my mind. I looked wildly to Grant and was reassured to find him smiling.

"They're here," he said unnecessarily. "Shall we welcome them to our home?" He smiled down at me encouragingly. "Everything will be fine. Just remember. Don't make them too comfortable. They'll leave that much sooner."

I only had time to shake my head in disgust at his tactless remark before the hall was filled with people all talking at once and enough baggage spread around the floor for a two-month stay.

I glimpsed a petite figure detach itself from the main group and head for Grant. I tried to watch this reunion, but I was crushed in a tight hug. Smothered in a cloud of lavender water, I was kissed on both cheeks. A voice spoke in my ear.

"You must be Grant's wife. My dear, I'm so happy to meet you. I've wanted that young man to marry for years." I was released, but the soft voice continued, "Where is he? Where is that handsome nephew of mine?"

I watched Celia Whitmore grab Grant in a tight embrace. I

was freed to stare into eyes as blue and frosty as my husband's. He looked me over critically. His lips pursed in distaste.

"So you're Grant's wife. Huh!" he snorted. "At least you don't look like a trollop!"

My mouth dropped open in shock and outrage. Before I had a chance to tell him what I thought, he had turned away to speak to Raymond.

"You'll have to excuse my husband," said a soft voice at my shoulder.

I turned to find Helene. I started to smile and offer her a warm welcome, but the words stuck in my throat.

"We're all hurt that Grant would choose to leave Whitmore Halls. I can't for the life of me see any attraction here." Her hostile brown eyes raked me, much as the old man's had.

I could feel my cheeks redden, but I held my tongue. "Grant," I called, interrupting his reunion with Celia, "let's go into the study. We'll be more comfortable there." I led the way, taking a chair near the windows.

From here I was afforded a view of everyone. Unobtrusively I watched them all, sorting out their individual personalities. Before forming an opinion of them, I had to take into account their remarks in the hall. Outside of Celia, I wasn't the reason for this visit. Grant was the attraction.

Arthur Whitmore's overbearing ways dominated any room he was in. In his younger days, I was sure, he'd been a handsome man. Age and ill health had stooped his shoulders and slowed his step. His feet shuffled along, with him relying on the aid of a cane. His head was covered with a heavy thatch of white hair, but his eyes were just as sharp as a young man's. I knew. I'd already experienced his penetrating glare.

Celia sat on the edge of her chair, her eyes darting from her brother to Grant. She seemed to be expecting some sort of clash between the two men. Her eyes were very brown, as was her hair, though it was salted rather heavily with gray. Her build was sturdy and might have been considered rather dowdy if it hadn't been for her noble stance. I'd long ago decided this was a trait inherited from generation to generation. All the Whitmores moved with a pride that was very deep-rooted.

I observed Arthur and Celia, but I was drawn to Helene. Not as one friend to another but as an adversary. I wasn't sure why I felt this way so soon after meeting. Outside of her opening remark to me, she had ignored me completely.

Helene was perched daintily on the arm of her chair. Soft blond curls framed her pretty face. Her eyes were the color of molasses. Her yellow hair and brown eyes reminded me of a brown-eyed Susan, a flower that grows wild in this part of the country.

I leaned back in my chair, content to let Grant do the entertaining. Only it wasn't my husband who began the polite conversation.

Helene had kept her warm eyes on Grant from the moment we had settled in the study. Her pink mouth was drawn into a grimace. "Grant, darling. I . . . We have missed you. Why in the world have you decided to live way off down here at the end of nowhere?"

Grant grinned at her indulgently. "For one thing, Helene, we're upriver from New Orleans, and St. Louis is hardly the end of nowhere."

"You know what I mean," she pouted prettily. "You're so far away from your family."

I had hoped to be forgotten, but Grant didn't let that happen. He came to sit next to me. I looked up at him. What's he up to? I wondered to myself. I didn't have long to wait. He got right to the point.

"I believe you can all see my reasons. I have a very wonderful woman, who's become my wife. We have a fine home here that has been in her family for generations." I felt the pressure of his hand on my shoulder. I looked up at him. The light in his eyes surprised me.

He sighed most convincingly. "My only regret is her father died before he saw us married." Grant ran a single finger down the length of my cheek. "He wanted us to marry. It was his last request. I'm sorry he can't know how happy we are."

I reached up and took his hand from my cheek. I kept a firm hold of his wayward hand. To our audience, I was sure, we looked the loving couple. The fact was I gave his hand a tight squeeze of warning. I didn't think he needed to be quite so free with his caresses. If I hadn't known better, I might have believed Grant's words. He was good. In fact, he should have been on the stage rather than wasting his talents on his cattle. This thought brought a secret smile to my lips.

Helene noted my smile and bristled. "I never thought to see you so smitten, Grant. She must have you under a spell." Softly Helene added under her breath, "Or curse!"

Aunt Celia clicked her tongue in disapproval. I chose to ignore Helene's barbed remark. I could feel the hostility in the room and, to my amazement, most of it was directed at me.

"Bah!" snorted the old man. He pounded his walking stick on the floor. All eyes turned to him. "You talk of doing as her father wished, but what of me? Why did you pick this place to raise my grandchildren? You had a perfectly good home. If you had to marry this girl, why didn't you bring her back to the Halls?"

"We've only been married a few weeks," said Grant.

"So," he grumbled, "how long were you going to wait?" Before Grant could say anything, Arthur looked around him critically. "Seems to be a well-built house, but it can't compare with the Halls. Why you would throw your life away on this is more than I can understand."

I could feel the muscles bunching in the arm Grant had pressed at my side. He was tensing for battle. I knew if I let him speak it would only goad the old man into an argument.

Not giving Grant the chance to reply, I soothed over the situation. "I'm sure your home is special to you, just as mine is to me. I'm fortunate Grant feels about Willowcrest as I do. We hope to make it a very fine place one day."

I came to my feet saying, "And now I'll show you to your rooms. I'm sure you'd like to freshen up before dinner. You even have time for a short nap, if you like. Dinner is at six. Grant and I take time for a small drink before we go into the dining room."

Playing the grand lady, I swept elegantly from the room. "Follow me, please," I directed. "I've put you in the green room, Aunt Celia." I smiled at her and added, "May I call you that?"

"I'd like nothing better, my dear," she assured me.

Helene sniffed, "Don't call me Mrs. Whitmore. That sounds like an old woman, which I'm not. Call me Helene."

I nodded. "Thank you, and I'm Althea to you both." I turned to Helene. "I wasn't sure what room you and your husband would prefer, so I'll leave that up to you."

Celia went into her room, saying she thought my suggestion of a nap a fine one. That left Helene and me alone. I showed her all the rooms, but she was undecided. She pointed to the last room on the right.

"What room is that?"

"That's the master bedroom," I said coolly.

"I see," she murmured. "I think the room next to it will be fine for me." She raised her head to look at me. "Art and I haven't shared a bed since our marriage. He's in such pain, poor man. The room across there will suit his needs."

I directed John with the baggage, then started to the bedroom I was to share with Grant. Helene stopped me with a question.

"Grant's leg has improved. Doesn't he limp anymore?"

Something in her tone caused me to look at her. I was trying to understand her words, or was it what she *wasn't* saying that troubled me?

"He's doing fine," I said simply.

"Does it bother you to be married to a cripple?" she asked.

Sharp words were on the tip of my tongue, but I asked her a question instead. "Is that the way you see Grant?"

Helene fluffed her bright hair. I thought she was going to ignore my question, but she finally said, "At one time we were very close to each other. I think he loved me, but after his accident I was afraid I might not be strong enough to be his wife."

"Really," I murmured, my eyes on her. "Was that the real reason? Or was it you were afraid he might not be enough of a man for you?"

She faced me. Her eyes cold and calculating. "You don't know what you're talking about."

"But I can guess," I murmured.

I don't know where our conversation might have led if Grant and his father hadn't come up the stairs. Helene gave me a very chilly look before going into her bedroom. I went into the master bedroom, pondering our short talk. It might have been short, but it was to the point.

My thoughts were interrupted as Grant came into the room. For the moment, we were hidden from prying eyes. He saw my cheeks flushed in anger and asked, "What were you and Helene talking about?"

"It wasn't important," I lied.

"It must have been interesting," he commented.

"*I* didn't think so." To change the subject, I said, "You really are a fine actor. Your performance downstairs was worthy of an award."

He bowed. "Thank you. You should get into the spirit of the thing. It could be fun."

"I haven't found the right opportunity," I said cautiously. "When I do, remember, it's just an act. I don't want you to become a conceited oaf from all the nice things I'll be saying." Grant only laughed heartily.

It was time to dress for dinner and I wasn't sure where or

how to go about it. I was searching the corners of the room for some privacy when I felt Grant's eyes on me.

He said, "What are you looking for?"

"Nothing."

He pulled his shirt off and went to the washbasin to shave. I watched the strong muscles play across his back. I smothered a sigh of appreciation before unhooking my gown. All I really needed to do was change my dress. I let the soiled one fall to the floor. Underneath I wore the soft filmy undergarments that had been sent with my wedding dress. I knew Grant was watching. Some devil inside of me made me turn around so he was rewarded with a full frontal view. I put my hands on my hips and took a deep breath, knowing how my rounded breasts filled the material. I couldn't meet his eyes, but a sudden flush of modesty made me reach for my robe. Once it was wrapped securely around me, I pointed to the wall separating our room from Helene's.

"Helene's in that room," I whispered.

Grant shrugged and turned back to his shaving. "Should that concern me?"

"Do you think she can hear us?"

"I doubt it. Why?" He turned to me suspiciously.

"But if she can, don't you think she should hear us enjoying ourselves?" I smiled at him, raising my eyebrows, much as I'd seen him do.

Grant took a step toward me, wiping the lather from his chin. "What do you have in mind?" he said softly.

I moved nimbly out of his reach but giggled loudly. "Grant darling," I cooed, "we haven't time for that now. You might wrinkle my dress." I grinned playfully. In a whisper I asked, "How is this for playacting, darling?"

His blue eyes narrowed. Suddenly he lunged for me, bringing me up tight against his chest. My robe parted and our bare skin touched. I caught my breath. His mouth quickly covered mine, cutting off my cry of surprise. I ran my hands up his bare arms, enjoying the hardness of his muscles and the warmth of his lips.

Grant broke away, moving back to laugh in my face. "And my sweet wife, how was that for acting? Two can play your game."

I raised my hand to his face, but this time he was ready. His voice was low. "You got away with that once, my sweet. Not again." His playfulness was at an end. "Let's finish dressing."

I still tingled from his kiss. I had asked for it. I had teased him, but once again the joke was on me. I had outsmarted myself.

CHAPTER EIGHT

Dinner was a success that evening, as far as the food was concerned. For me, it was an ordeal to be endured. I pasted a smile on my face, but a lump was stuck in my throat. At last I was able to urge the others into the study while I took a minute to congratulate Agnes and her helpers on their work. I wasn't gone long, but in my absence, Arthur and Celia had retired to their rooms, leaving Grant and Helene alone.

I stood outside the door. I didn't have any intention of eavesdropping, but I heard my name mentioned.

"Althea is my wife," said Grant. He held a glass of brandy in his hand. I tried to see Helene, but she was out of my line of vision. Her voice came to me all too clearly.

"But darling, I know why you married her. She has a home you've fallen in love with. It isn't her you care for. It's this house. It's everything you've always wanted for Whitmore

Halls. I know how much you've wanted to change its dark and cheerless rooms." She moved to stand closer to Grant. Now she could plead with him, her hand on his arm. "Come back to us. Together you and I can change Arthur's mind. We will make him listen to your plans."

Grant stared down at her, shaking his head. "It's more than the rooms. I almost wish it were that simple. This is my home now. I want to live here." His voice filled with scorn as he asked, "How is my father? Your husband."

Helene blushed but kept her eyes on Grant's face. "He's all right, I suppose, for a man his age. He's in pain all the time."

She lowered her eyes shyly so she could look up coyly. "We've never lived together as husband and wife, Grant." When Grant didn't say anything, she pouted. "I know you don't understand why I married Arthur, but I had to. You were hurt, crippled." Her voice trembled over the word, but she swallowed and hurried on. "I didn't know if I could look after you. I knew you would need help. I wasn't sure if I could give it."

Grant laughed bitterly. "I see. So instead of looking after me, you chose to marry my father. A man almost three times your age and crippled with rheumatism." He shook his head scornfully. "You expect me to believe that?"

Tears were in her voice as she held out her hands. "Had I known you would get well, I'd have followed you anywhere. Can't you see how upset I was? I didn't know what to do. You left the Halls. I had to do something. When your father asked me to marry him, it seemed like a solution. I needed a home and money. He had both." She rubbed her cheek on his sleeve. "I've missed you. I'd give up everything I have today if we could have a life together."

A small smile played across Grant's lips. I wanted to see into his eyes, but I was too far away. I listened breathlessly for his answer. When it came, it didn't give me any relief.

"What's done is done. You're married. So am I. We both have separate lives."

"But, my darling, it doesn't have to be that way. Arthur is more like a father to me. I need a real man. I want to be with you."

I'd heard enough. This time I didn't wait for Grant's answer. I turned and ran quietly up to the bedroom. But I couldn't take comfort from the room. It wasn't my room. It was Grant's. I paced the floor angrily. How dare he not tell me of his involvement with Helene. I had a right to know before she came into my house.

Why hadn't Grant come right out and said he wasn't interested in Helene? I was afraid I knew the answer. His mouth might say he had a life of his own, but I was sure his heart was aching for the petite blonde.

Helene had been his reason for anxiety before their arrival. He'd been afraid to see her again. Afraid of what he might feel for her. His father's wife. But I couldn't see her as such, though the law fully recognized her marriage. Arthur did seem like her father.

I stopped my pacing to sit on the edge of the bed. What a terrible twist of fate. I was in love with Grant. He was my husband. I wasn't going to give him up without a fight.

Thoughts of the jewels being used to entice Grant away were a thing of the past. I would continue to hunt for them but only because they were a part of Father's legacy.

As I undressed I wondered how I could win Grant's love. At least I had a better understanding of the situation. I knew who my foe was. I also had an advantage over Helene. I was Grant's wife. I could act kind and loving. Grant would be expecting something of that sort from me. What I was counting on was his enjoyment of my attention. Why *shouldn't* he fall in love with me? I had improved my appearance. I had just as lovely an assortment of clothes as Helene. I chose to ignore the fact that she was tiny and seemingly helpless, while I was tall, long-legged and very capable of standing on my own two feet. It all depended on what Grant liked in his women. I prayed I had read his character correctly.

I put on my old flannel nightgown after hesitating over a soft silky blue one. I might flirt and tease Grant, but I wasn't going to use my body as bait. I wanted Grant. I wanted him to desire me, but I didn't want him making love to my body but seeing Helene's face. I had to be sure of his feelings for me. Then we would progress to the intimate part of our marriage.

I planned to be in bed asleep when Grant came up the stairs. Though I was in bed, the light remained on. I heard his step outside the door and hurried to blow out the flame. I was too slow. He came in just as I leaned over the lamp.

He looked at me in a strange manner. "Leave it," he muttered.

I lay back against the pillows, pulling the covers up to my chin. I closed my eyes but strained to hear every sound as Grant walked around the room. He was in that odd mood of his. I wondered what he was thinking and longed to ask. His mouth was pursed in a hard bitter line. I didn't know what to say. I almost didn't say anything. Then, very simply, I called, "Good night."

He swung around to leer at me. "Don't I get a wifely kiss?"

"I don't think so. I'm too tired for games." I snuggled deeper under the covers.

He glared at me a moment longer. "Is that why you didn't come back to the study?"

I opened my eyes to meet his. I looked away. "No. I came to the door, but I decided you and Helene might wish to have a moment of privacy."

I ached to shout accusations to him but knew that would only start a terrible argument, which I didn't have the stomach for. I gave all evidence of not caring. I was ready to go to sleep. It was several minutes before I heard him blow out the lights. I lay tense and waiting. The bed shook from his weight.

A cool draft of air blew across my warm body as he lifted the covers. My muscles bunched nervously. He didn't touch me. He didn't say a word. I lay there on my back, my eyes wide open.

It was difficult to lay quietly at Grant's side. I wanted to toss and turn, but I just listened to his slow, even breathing. Very soon I could tell he was asleep. I was able to relax. This time I closed my eyes and drifted off to sleep.

I awoke from a sound sleep to hear angry voices. I stirred slowly, opening my eyes to find myself staring into Grant's laughing blue ones. I moved back quickly, embarrassed to find I'd slept the night away pressed tightly against him, an arm flung over his back.

Grant grinned widely and would have moved closer if the voices hadn't risen in volume. He frowned, listening quietly.

"What is going on?" I asked.

He threw back the covers, giving me a brief flash of tanned skin before pulling on his pants. "I don't know," he snapped. "But I sure as hell will find out!" He adjusted his tight-fitting trousers around his naked waist. "It's too early for all these arguments."

Suddenly loud screams filled the air. Grant was out the door and down the hall before I could shrug into my robe. I followed more slowly. Raymond stood in the doorway of Arthur's room. I could hear Grant shouting orders. Raymond gave a curt nod of his head and ran down the stairs, calling over his shoulder, "I'll have the doctor back as quickly as I can."

Hearing the word "doctor," I feared the worst. I quickly entered Arthur's room to see if I could be of help.

Grant was kneeling over the still figure of his father. Helene was sobbing on Celia's shoulder. Celia Whitmore's face had aged since I'd last seen her. She stood pale and trembling. Absently she stroked Helene's hair, but her eyes were on Grant's face.

"Is he still alive?" she asked fervently.

Grant glanced up. "Barely." He touched his father's hand. "It'll take Raymond a while to get back. We have to get Father on the bed. Give me a hand," he directed.

Helene turned to Grant, crying, "I can't touch him. He's dying. Dying!" Her voice rose hysterically.

Grant moved quickly. He grabbed Helene by the shoulders and shook her until her head snapped back and forth on her limber neck. "Stop that!" he said. "He isn't dead. You can either help us or go back to your room."

Her brown eyes filled with fresh tears. "I can't," she choked. "I can't touch that dreadful old man." Sobbing, she ran from the room.

Grant looked after her, unsure whether he should follow her. Duty won out. He turned back to his father. Celia and I helped move Arthur. I smoothed the covers over his unmoving body. His chest could scarcely be seen rising and falling with each labored breath.

Grant motioned for us to follow him to the far side of the bedroom. He asked fiercely, "What happened in here this morning?"

I started to say he should be questioning Helene, but one look from his cold eyes silenced my lips.

Celia shook her head. Her eyes were on her brother. I turned to look at him too. His face was pasty but his lips were blue. It looked as if the whole left side of his face was distorted. It was like looking through a wavy mirror. His mouth was pulled down in an exaggerated droop. Saliva drooled out the corner. He still wore his nightcap. It had become dislodged, now sitting at an odd angle.

"Well?" repeated Grant.

Celia's voice trembled. She looked ready to collapse herself. "I was asleep when I heard Arthur call Helene's name. I didn't know she was in his room. I went to see what he wanted. When I opened the door, Helene was standing at the foot of his bed. I started to leave when I heard Arthur saying terrible things to her."

"What things?" demanded Grant.

Celia glanced at me and shook her head. "I'd rather not say."

"Do you want me to leave?" I asked.

"No," said Grant firmly. "Go ahead, Aunt Celia. What did Father have to say?"

"He accused Helene of starting trouble for the two of you. He told Helene to leave Althea alone. Helene got mad. They screamed at each other." Celia shuddered. "I tried to get them to stop, but Arthur was like a wild person. He got out of bed and took Helene's arm. He shook her dreadfully. Then he grabbed at his chest and fell."

Celia turned sorrow-filled eyes to her nephew. "I knew he had a heart condition. It was my fault this happened. I was supposed to keep him quiet." She sank into a chair, covering her face with her hands. "I should have made him get back in bed and rest."

Grant rubbed a weary hand over his face. He walked back to his father's bed. I looked down at the old woman sitting huddled in the chair. Pity for her brought tears to my eyes. I heard her mumbling. I leaned closer so I could hear.

"He guessed. I know he has."

I didn't know what she meant, but I patted her shoulder in comfort. She looked up at me. Her eyes seemed to focus past my shoulder. She didn't even see me standing at her side.

Softly I tried to reassure her. "Don't blame yourself."

Grant agreed. "That's right, Auntie. I know how Father is, especially when he loses his temper. You couldn't have gotten him back in bed."

Celia stared at me. She shook her head sharply, as if ridding herself of old dreams. She spoke softly. "He's been doing so well. He got it into his head to visit you after I told you had married and settled down here. I made the mistake of saying I didn't think it would be a good idea to visit. He flew into a rage. I finally had to agree just so he would rest. Now this had to happen."

I suggested softly to Grant, "I think she should lie down."

"Yes," he murmured absently. "Yes, of course. It'll be a while before the doctor can come. I'll stay with Father. You both go get dressed." As an afterthought, he added, "Althea, check on Helene. See if she's all right. She's had a terrible shock."

This was the last thing I wanted to do, but Celia wasn't able to cope with Helene. I nodded my agreement, then walked Celia to her room. After I got her settled, I knocked on Helene's door.

A muffled voice called, "Come in."

Once inside the door, I knew at once I was the last person Helene had expected. Her hair had been freshly combed, and there was a new application of makeup on her pale cheeks. Her other nightdress had been changed for a more seductive one. She lay on the bed, an arm tossed mournfully over her forehead. Her eyes were closed. She was the picture of a grieving woman.

I knew it was mean, but I couldn't help myself. I clapped my hands together, whispering softly, "Bravo. What a touching performance."

Her brown eyes flew open. With it came a flash of disappointment. Her first words confirmed what I'd suspected.

"Where's Grant?" she demanded.

"With his father," I said. "I came to see if you needed anything."

With an exasperated sigh, she got up from the bed. Picking up a brush, she attacked her hair viciously. When she didn't answer me, I said, "If there isn't anything, I have to go get dressed and back to my husband."

Helene glared at me. She looked with contempt at my modest high-necked nightgown and simple robe. Neither could begin to compare with her own silken ensemble. Her voice was full of scorn as she asked, "Is that what you wear to bed? Don't you think Grant would prefer something a bit more feminine?"

I raised my eyebrows questioningly. "Really," I replied, "I wouldn't know. He's never said. I just have his actions to go by. Last night he didn't seem to mind what I wore. It was off so quickly." I didn't wait to see her reaction to my words. I turned and closed her bedroom door with a snap.

I dressed quickly, my anger spurring me on. How dare she question what I wear to bed? She had her nerve, acting like she cared about Arthur when all the time she was setting a trap for Grant.

I put my anger behind me when I went back to Arthur's room. Grant sat hunched in a chair, his head in his hands. He looked up as I came in.

"The doctor should be here soon," I said softly.

"He might be too late."

"Don't talk that way. You've said your father is a tough old bird. He'll live just to spite you."

Grant grinned. "That might be true."

We sat waiting for the doctor's arrival. We didn't speak. There was nothing to say. I was sure Grant was remembering some of his arguments with his father. I hoped he was also remembering some of the good times as well. I didn't want to intrude on his memories.

I was the first to notice a change in Arthur's breathing. I called it to Grant's attention. We both went to the bed. I picked up a cloth and gently wiped his face. His eyes fluttered open and darted wildly around the room. His mouth gaped open as he tried to talk.

"Shh," I said. "Rest. Don't try to talk. The doctor has been sent for."

His eyes pierced mine, searching for something. I smiled, wanting to convey a feeling of confidence and tranquility. Grant spoke rather gruffly. I sensed it was from emotion.

"Are you in pain, Father? Do you need anything?"

Arthur closed his eyes but opened them quickly. He tried to speak. He seemed almost frantic to get across a message to us.

"What does he want?" I murmured.

"I don't know," said Grant.

Arthur's eyes turned from me to Grant, then back to me again. Slowly he closed his eyes and relaxed.

"Is he dead?" I asked in concern, remembering how relaxed Papa had gotten when he breathed his last.

"No," said Grant after listening to Arthur's chest. "I guess he's unconscious." He moved back from the bed to pace the room. "I wish the doctor would get here!"

"I'm here," said a dry voice from the door.

I turned to see the man who'd taken care of Papa. I felt embarrassed that he'd overheard Grant's remark, but apparently neither he nor Grant minded. The doctor ushered me out the door.

I stood in the hall staring at the door, wondering why I'd suddenly been evicted. Behind me Helene spoke.

"How is he?"

Looking at her, I couldn't keep the disapproval from my face. She was dressed all in black. Nodding at her clothing, I said, "Isn't this a bit premature?"

She shrugged, unconcerned with what I thought. "I'm not in mourning yet," she said. "Black just suits my mood this morning."

Celia came out of her room, forestalling more barbed remarks between Helene and me. Concern for her brother was written on her face.

"I heard the doctor's buggy. How is Arthur?"

"The doctor has started his examination." I didn't like the paleness of her face. Her gait was unsteady, so I helped her into a nearby chair. "We all have to pray he'll be fine." I looked at Helene as I said this. She chose to ignore me.

Celia clasped her hands together in her lap. "I need to speak to Arthur. I hope he'll be conscious soon."

"He regained consciousness for a minute when Grant and I were by his bed."

I thought I saw a flash of uneasiness cross Celia's face. Then it was gone. All I could see was hope. "Did he ask for me? Why didn't you come and get me?"

"He can't speak, Celia," I explained gently. "I know he was trying to tell us something, but he can't form the words. Something has happened to his tongue and mouth."

"Does he understand what has happened to him?"

"I don't know." I tried to explain what I'd seen in his eyes. "Something is bothering him. I don't know Arthur well, but the look in his eyes told me he had something on his mind."

Helene spoke for the first time. "If he can't speak, how do you know something's bothering him?"

Impatiently I repeated, "I said it was a look in his eyes. I can't explain it any better than that. I *do* know that Grant noticed it too."

Helene smoothed the soft material of her dress, stretching it tightly across her full bosom. "I think the doctor made a useless trip out from town."

For the first time, I caught a glimmer of the Whitmore temper in meek Aunt Celia. Her eyes flashed. "What a terrible thing to say, Helene. Don't let me hear you say anything like that again! Arthur's been good to you. He's your husband, or have you forgotten?"

"How could I? It was the biggest mistake I've ever made. I can't forget I'm married to him. You never let me. You're always reminding me that I'm married to the old goat."

Celia didn't reprimand her again, but her eyes still smoldered.

It was an ill-at-ease group that waited for the doctor to tell us about Arthur. Helene paced the floor, acting as if Arthur was being ill just to inconvenience her. At last the bedroom door opened. In utter fascination, I watched the scene that unfolded before me. As if on cue, Helene's lovely face crumpled into a mask of misery. She hurried to Grant, clinging to his arm.

In a forlorn voice, she cried, "Will he be all right?"

Grant didn't answer but kept a comforting arm around her waist. The doctor spoke honestly to us all.

"He's in a grave condition. He's suffered a massive stroke, paralyzing his entire left side. I can't be sure at this early date if it's a permanent condition, but he'll need rest and plenty of quiet. He's not to be provoked. Just keep him still, and the next few weeks will tell us how severe the damage is. I'll send out a lady from town to help take care of him."

"When will she arrive?" I asked.

"This evening," he said.

"In the meantime what should we do to make him comfortable?" I questioned, as no one else said anything.

"You're used to the sickroom, my dear. Treat him much as you did your own father. The nurse will take over afterward."

So I was to be given charge of the patient. I looked to Grant and saw he expected me to do as the doctor said. I nodded my head and went back to Arthur's room. I felt irritated. But who else was there to take charge? I couldn't see Helene bathing Arthur's head. More likely she would drown the poor old man. Celia would do it, but she wasn't really up to caring for herself. I was all that was left until the woman came from town.

I was surprised to find Arthur awake. His eyes brightened as I approached the bed. I spoke softly. "You should be resting."

He tried to smile, but it was a gruesome twisting of his misshapen mouth. He grunted deep in his throat.

"Don't try to talk. I'll do the talking. You just rest. Sarah will bring up some broth soon. I'm sure you're hungry." I watched him close his eyes, then open them quickly.

Suspiciously I asked, "Does that mean yes?" He closed his eyes again. "How wonderful," I said. "How smart of you to think of this. Are you in pain?" His eyes blinked. "Good," I smiled.

Sarah brought in the broth and I tied a napkin under his chin. We spilled more than he ate, but I think at last he was satisfied. I stood up to move the tray away, but feeble fingers grabbed at my skirt. I turned to him and said, "What is it, Arthur? Are you still hungry?"

He didn't close his eyes, so I laid down the tray. Gently but firmly I pried his fingers loose and tucked his hand under the covers. "I'm going to set your tray outside the door. I'm not leaving." Somehow this seemed to set his mind at rest. He closed his eyes. They stayed closed this time. He slipped off to sleep.

I put the tray outside the door, then went back to sit at his side. I was puzzled by the man's actions. Yesterday he'd treated me with contempt. Yet today he didn't want me out of his sight.

What had happened this morning? Somehow I thought it was more than Celia had said. She seemed awfully distraught. What had she mumbled this morning? "He knows. He's guessed." What had she been talking about? Her eyes had looked so wild. Had I glimpsed terror? Who or what did Celia fear?

I shook my head, feeling frustrated. I'd been such a fool to worry about marrying Grant. I was finding marriage to him quite simple. It was his family that brought me more worry and problems. Had I known what I did now, I would have run from Grant and Willowcrest. I thought of Grant and his strong warm arms and gentle passionate lips and reconsidered. No. I wouldn't have run from him. I was where I wanted to be. My feelings were confirmed as I watched my husband enter the room.

Grant had taken the time to shave and put on clean clothes. He greeted me with a warm kiss. I wondered at his action but turned to find Arthur's knowing eye on us. I thought I could detect a gleam in them.

"What do you think of my wife now, Father?" said Grant cheerfully. "Is she taking good care of you?"

Arthur closed his eyes, then opened them quickly. I explained what I'd discovered. Grant grinned. "So you and he have been talking?"

I chuckled. "I've been doing all the talking. Arthur's just been listening."

I watched Arthur's eyes dart back and forth between Grant and me. He gurgled something, but I couldn't begin to understand. Somehow Grant sensed what was on his father's mind. He put his arm around me, drawing me up close. "You like Althea, don't you?" Arthur closed his eyes. "You can understand why I married her?" Again his eyes closed. "And you don't mind her bearing your grandchildren?"

I stiffened at his remark but kept a smile on my lips. Arthur seemed to be enjoying this ridiculous conversation. I'd had enough. I turned my back to the old man on the pretext of smoothing my husband's collar. Through clenched teeth, I muttered, "What are you doing? All of this is unnecessary."

"I love you too, dearest," Grant said rather loudly, planting a kiss on my neck.

I shivered, closing my eyes. His nearness left me breathless. I cleared my throat. "You could be getting yourself into trouble. He's to be here for some time. What if he demands I get pregnant? Then what will you do?"

I sat back, smiling brightly in Grant's dark face. I'd turned the tables on him. Putting my face close to his, I said, "Smile, darling. Those were words of love I was whispering to you."

Grant did smile, but his eyes remained icy. "Why don't you go for a walk, my love. I'll stay here and keep Father company."

I was relieved. I waved good-bye to Arthur and hurried from the room. I needed to get away from Grant and into the fresh air. I only took time to grab a shawl from my room before going out the front door.

My feet took me around the house to the garden. Here I picked a simple bouquet to take up to the cemetery. I arranged the flowers in a vase and set it near the stone. The deep purple of the lilacs looked lovely next to the pink marble.

The air smelled clean. I hated the thought of going back to the house. It wasn't the house but the people inside that kept me walking. I couldn't get Helene out of my mind. It wasn't her attraction for Grant that I thought about. I wondered why she felt she had to marry Arthur when Grant left Whitmore Halls. Surely with her youth and beauty, there would have been younger men. Why had she settled for the old man? Was it a chance to always be near Grant?

I felt as if I'd come into the theater in the middle of the first act. I could recognize the actors, but the plot was confusing. I had questions but few answers. Grant didn't think I need concern myself. Helene might answer me, but could I trust what she told me? I didn't think so. She saw only what she wanted to. Arthur couldn't speak. That left Celia. She seemed the most likely one to shed some light on what I wanted to know.

My wanderings had taken me along the path that led down to the river. I stood on the high bluff looking down at the lazy river. Its muddy water was deceiving. It looked peaceful, but I'd seen it whirling, pitching and destroying everything in its path. The gentle lapping of the water at the edge of the bank was almost mesmerizing. I felt soothed and relaxed. Perhaps I was too relaxed or I might have realized I was in danger. My only clue that I wasn't alone was the sharp crack of a stick. I turned, catching a brief flash of green before hands shoved me in the middle of my back.

As I rolled down the embankment, pebbles gouged into my soft arms. Dirt got in my eyes, blinding me. My hands fought for something to grab hold of. But I was spinning too fast. Then abruptly I stopped.

I lay quietly. I felt bruised and scraped all over. I moved my legs first, and though they ached they did work. I sat up but closed my eyes weakly as the world tilted at a crazy angle. My arms burned from the many scratches. Blood ran down from a cut on my head. I used the tail of my dress to wipe the dirt and blood from my eyes. When I could I looked around me. A spindly oak tree had kept me from hurling off the edge of the bluff to an outcropping of rocks below. I closed my eyes, sick to my stomach at my narrow escape.

I had to gather my strength. I was frightened. Someone had pushed me. I was afraid they might be waiting up above to finish the job. I looked back the way I'd come. I couldn't see or hear anyone, but I remained where I was for a time.

I didn't know how much time had passed, but I knew I had to get back to the house. I climbed carefully, afraid I might slip and fall backward. I broke my fingernails clutching at rocks and weeds.

Tears streamed down my face as I pulled myself back over the edge. In the distance I could see Willowcrest. It looked good to me. As I had rolled down that embankment, I feared never to see it again.

It was a slow trip back to the house. I stumbled, almost falling several times. By the time I got to the front door, I was shivering from fear and pain. Every shadow or noise sent me into near hysteria. I knew someone had tried to kill me.

I got the front door open with the last of my strength and almost frightened John to death. He dropped the tray he was carrying and began to shout for Grant. I didn't wait to see what happened next. I was home. I fainted for the first time in my life.

CHAPTER NINE

When I came to, I was lying on the bed. Grant was sitting at my side. I struggled to a sitting position. "I was pushed," I blurted out. Tears filled my eyes.

He put his hands on my shoulders, trying to press me back against the pillows. "Rest," he commanded. "You're here now."

"But I was pushed. Down by the river."

"You were probably standing too close to the edge," he said.

I pulled away from him so I could look into his eyes. I shook my head. "I felt the hands shove me, Grant. I didn't slip. I heard a twig snap, like someone had stepped on it. I turned to see who it was, but before I could, someone pushed me and I fell." As I remembered how helpless it had felt rolling down that bluff, I shivered. "It was terrible. I might have been killed."

I could see the disbelief in his eyes. "Why won't you believe what I'm saying?" I demanded. "I heard this twig snap. I saw a flash of—" I stopped. My eyes widened in horror as I noticed what Grant wore. I recoiled from his green jacket.

"What is it, Althea?" he asked in concern.

I tried to speak, but my mouth might as well have been filled with cotton. I finally turned from him, shaking my head. I don't know what he would have said or done if Sarah hadn't come to bathe my wounds.

He got up from the bed. "If you think I should call the doctor, I'll send Raymond for him."

I shook my head. There was no need to bring him out twice in one day. Grant stared at me a moment longer, then shook his head in bewilderment at my unusual behavior. As the door closed behind Grant, I closed my eyes, letting Sarah dress my cuts.

I seemed to be resting, but my mind was very active. I knew I'd been pushed. I could still feel the pressure at the small of my back where the hands had come in contact. I thought of Grant's disbelief and of his green jacket. Would he try to hurt or kill me? With Arthur so ill and me out of the way, he and Helene would have a chance for a life together. Or was it Helene who had crept up behind me? Somehow the deed was more in keeping with her character.

I stayed in bed that evening and all the next day. I was stiff and sore, but my scratches weren't anything serious. The one on my head was the worst. I experimented arranging my hair and found a way to cover the cut with a curl.

Grant showed concern for me, but he treated the incident lightly. He had told everyone I'd slipped and fell. Rather than call my husband a liar, I'd gone along with him. It was referred to as "my accident." But it hadn't been an accident. I was jumpy and edgy. When someone knocked on the bedroom door, I watched it open with dread. It was a terrible feeling to distrust everyone. Helene and Grant were my prime suspects, but there were others too. Raymond, Celia and all the servants. The only one outside my suspicions was Arthur.

His nurse had arrived the evening of my fall. It wasn't until the next afternoon that I met her. She was a plain woman but strong as an ox. She had the muscles needed to turn or move Arthur when he needed his position changed. She also tolerated no nonsense in regard to her patient. She kept a close eye on his visitors and how Arthur responded to them. It was the nurse who forbade Helene from entering the sickroom. He had shown great agitation toward his wife. I'd also been told he'd been restless ever since my accident. I went to see him as soon as I was able. I even tried to laugh over my clumsiness. Maybe it was my imagination, but Arthur watched me closely.

What did he know? I wondered, then dismissed the thought. What could he know? He was bedfast, unable to leave the room. He had developed a liking for me. Giving his nurse a brief supper break, I stayed with him, reading aloud. When she returned I went downstairs. I was thinking about taking a short stroll close to the house when Helene came bubbling out of the study.

Her brown eyes danced with excitement. "Do you know what that darling man has promised me?" She didn't wait for my answer but continued, "He's taking me to town tomorrow. While I shop he has some business to do. Afterward he's taking me to dinner and the theater." She looked at me in triumph. Her looked seemed to say, "So there."

I didn't give her the satisfaction of seeing how peeved I was. Her feet danced past me and to the stairs. Here she stopped to say, "I have to go see to my clothes. I want to look just perfect for Grant."

My eyes followed her twisting figure up the stairs. I knew I had a wicked gleam in my eye. I turned to find myself face to face with Grant.

He was grinning. "I thought that would cheer her up."

My voice was dry as I said, "I didn't realize she needed cheering."

"She's been upset this last day or so," he said. Looking down at me, he added, "You don't look very pleased. I thought you loved the theater."

"I didn't realize I was to be included," I snapped.

Grant smiled lazily before slipping an arm around my waist. "But of course, my pet. I couldn't squire her all over town alone. People would talk. This way with you along, as chaperone, it'll all be innocent." He chuckled in my ear. "You weren't jealous, were you?"

I jerked away, raising my nose in the air. "Why should I be

jealous?" I tried to act unconcerned, but an excited grin sneaked past my reserve. "You'll have to excuse me too. I have to go check my wardrobe."

I spent the rest of that day and the next afternoon grooming myself for our outing. I knew whatever Helene wore, it would be very feminine and daring. I couldn't hope to compete with her daintiness, so I didn't try. I chose a gown that was elegant and suited to my looks.

I had dressed and was on my way downstairs when I heard voices from the hall below. I looked over the edge and saw Helene dressed in pink. I'd been right about the daring of her dress. It had a very low neckline. From above, I saw an unrestricted view of bare flesh. I could well imagine what Grant was seeing, standing next to her.

"But darling," she cooed. "Why did you have to mention our trip into town to her? This would have been an ideal time for us to be together."

I stepped into sight, thereby stifling any more of Helene's complaints. I smiled as I moved toward them. "I hope I haven't kept you waiting. Sarah took longer with my hair." I took Grant's arm and pressed a light kiss to his surprised lips. I murmured provocatively, "Am I forgiven, darling?"

He stepped back to look me over carefully. Slowly he nodded his head. "When you look the way you do now, I could forgive you anything."

I felt warm and happy inside at his words. It made it easier for me to say graciously, "You look very lovely, Helene. I'm sure Grant will be the envy of every man we see tonight." I smiled into her furious eyes. I found I shouldn't have congratulated myself so soon on making her mad. She was a sly woman and found a way to get even with me.

Raymond had the carriage waiting for us out front. I was helped in first, followed by Helene, who took the seat across from me. She quickly swept her skirts to one side, smiling up invitingly at Grant.

"Sit here, Grant. Althea needs the extra room on her seat for her skirts. She won't want them wrinkled."

Grant looked where she pointed and saw my full skirts spread over the seat. Before I could tuck it away, he had sat down by Helene. I seethed inside. She was a sly cat. I had been underestimating her caginess. But no more. I would be ready the next time.

All the way into town, Helene chattered on about first one subject then another. Her questions were ridiculous as she tried to concentrate all of Grant's attention on herself. I sat quietly. My eyes stayed on the passing countryside. I tried to shut out Helene's voice, but it was too near at hand. I didn't know what Grant thought of her ceaseless prattle, but it infuriated me. I heaved a great sigh of relief when Raymond stopped at our destination.

Raymond helped Helene down, giving me a moment with Grant. I whispered angrily, "I hope you enjoyed her endless babbling. I have a headache from listening to her."

"What do you expect me to do?" he snapped.

"I don't know." I admitted, then added, "You might have said something to me."

"If you had worn a normal dress, I might have sat next to you." He glared at me. "You could have said something yourself. You just sat there, staring out the window. I could have used some help too."

So he needed some help, did he? I leaned forward so he could hear me clearly. "This isn't what you deserve, but I'll give you an apology." I'd been prepared to give him a light fleeting kiss. He saw what I had in mind and beat me at my own game. His arms wrapped around me, pulling me off the seat onto his lap. There on a main street of St. Louis, my husband kissed me with a passion I found electrifying. I melted against him, willing the kiss to go on forever, but it had to end. We separated breathlessly. I couldn't meet Grant's eyes. I didn't want to see their mocking glint.

I quickly stepped from the carriage and kept my back to it until I was sure it had disappeared down the street. I spoke to Helene. "I have an errand to do. I'll be back shortly." I didn't give her a chance to question me but almost ran down the street.

There was no errand. I couldn't face her. I needed time to sort out my feelings. Grant. I said his name, liking the way it felt on my tongue. I laughed inside, remembering a time not so long ago when his name had tasted bitter. I'd learned so much in such a short time.

I didn't have any place to go. Then I thought of Hilda. I had to see her. She would understand what was happening. I'd sent her a short note telling her of my marriage. Now that I'd made up my mind, I couldn't get to her small shop fast enough.

I was lucky to find her without a customer. She took me into the workroom, where she fixed me a cup of hot tea. It was like a dam bursting as the words came tumbling out. Hilda listened with kind sympathetic eyes, neither judging nor condemning me.

I told her the whole story except for Grant's green jacket and the flash of green I'd seen just as I was pushed. After tasting his last kiss, it was hard to picture him stealing up behind me. Could he kiss me tenderly while harboring thoughts of killing me? I didn't think so.

Hilda and I talked quietly, but she couldn't give me any answers. All she could give me was her friendship and a warning to be careful. I assured her I would. We parted with the promise I would send for her if I needed help. It felt good to know I wasn't completely at the mercy of Grant's family. I had someone too.

I'd been longer than planned. I couldn't find a hack to hire. I walked along briskly until I heard a shout. I turned to see Raymond parked across the street. With relief, I crossed and got in the Whitmore carriage. Raymond was waiting in front of the bank for Grant. I sat still, apprehensive but anxious to see Grant again. My thoughts brought a sparkle to my eyes and a rosy blush to my cheeks.

When Grant opened the door, his face registered his surprise. "What are you doing here?" he asked. "I thought you were with Helene."

I slid across the seat, making room for him next to me. "I went for a visit with Hilda. I was walking back when Raymond saw me."

He continued to stand in the doorway. His blue eyes were cool. He nodded to the vacant seat. "Wouldn't you rather I sat across from you? I wouldn't want to crush your gown."

I chuckled deeply. "That wasn't my idea, remember?" My smile was warm. I didn't want Grant to doubt his right to be at my side.

He sat down rather cautiously, puzzled by my behavior. It was only natural to take his arm and lean against him as the carriage pulled away from the curb. I kissed his ear lightly, feeling him freeze. I let my lips move from his ear to caress his cheek and settle on his lips. My hand rested intimately on his thigh.

Grant sat quietly, letting me tease him. Suddenly he grabbed my hand and forced me to turn so he could look into my eyes. I didn't want him to see my longing, but he tilted my chin up, forcing me to meet his eyes.

A small smile played around the corners of his mouth. He didn't say a word but pulled me into his arms. His lips found mine. This kiss was different from the others. I sensed an unleashed passion beneath his usual reserve. I knew I was sampling just a taste of the amorous traits my husband kept well hidden.

I trembled at his touch and yearned to be even closer than we were. Pressing against him, wanting him, I knew I was revealing my feelings. I was leaving myself open for a big hurt, but with his lips on mine I was past caring.

It was the slowing of the carriage that caused us to part. I waited for his smile. I hoped for kind loving words, but Grant turned away to stare out the window. I looked at his hair, loving the way it curled over the edge of his collar. I wanted to touch him again, but something in his manner rebuffed me. Hadn't he been stirred by our kiss? Hadn't he felt that wonderful flame of desire too? Though his breathing was slightly heavy, he behaved as before. Aloof and unaware of me at his side.

I might have questioned him, but Helene walked in. She took one look at us and sneered, "So this was your errand." She sat down in a huff. As I watched her, she quickly arranged her face into a petulant smile. Patting the seat next to her, she purred, "Darling, come sit here. I want you to point out all the sights for me. I don't wish to miss a thing."

I was surprised but tried to hide it when Grant picked up my hand. "I'm fine here, Helene. Althea assures me I won't harm her dress." He tucked my hand in his, dismissing Helene to stare out the window again. It was I who caught her cold glare.

I looked away, chilled. Helene was furious and that made me fear for my safety. I felt sure the danger came from her. I had to watch how far I provoked her. Her retaliation might be my demise. I had to stay alert.

Helene's bad humor remained all through our silent meal. Grant didn't say anything except to give our order to the waiter and to inquire if we needed anything more. I had nothing to say, though my mind was occupied. What was wrong with him? The meal was finished quickly. No titillating conversation prolonged the dismal affair.

When we arrived at the theater, we were early. Inadvertently Grant irritated Helene further. He sat down in the middle of the seat, forcing Helene and me to sit on each side of him. Helene didn't wish to share Grant's attention. She tried to brush me to one side, but Grant was firm. I smiled up at her serenely. With a glance full of hate, she flounced childishly out of the box.

"Where's she going?" demanded Grant. He started to get up to follow her. I was sure this was her plan when leaving the box, so I put out a detaining hand.

"Let her go," I said. "I'm sure she'll be right back. She must have wanted to see to her hair." I smiled up at him shyly. "I hope this play is as wonderful as the last one we saw. I enjoyed that evening very much."

For just a minute, his strange mood slipped away. He looked directly into my eyes, smiling. "I'm glad. It should have been an evening we both want to remember. I just wish . . ."

But he didn't get to finish. Helene came back giggling and flirting with a man in tow. I was furious at the interruption, then I saw who was with her. I stiffened as our eyes met. He was as handsome as I remembered. His gray eyes just as brazen as before. I felt them sweep over me, coming to rest on the low neck of my gown.

"So we meet again, Whitmore." He barely glanced at Grant but bowed low to me. "Hello, my dear. I've dreamed of you often since last we met. I hope you are well."

I jerked my hand back, not bothering to hide my distaste for him. Grant looked from my frozen face to the man's. He could see I was very upset. In a gruff voice, he said, "Who the hell are you?"

The man whirled around to stare at Grant. In surprise, he said, "You don't remember me?"

"Your face is familiar, but I can't place your name," admitted Grant.

The man continued to stare at Grant in disbelief. Finally he shook his head. "Sir, your memory is sadly lacking."

Grant's face hardened. Impatiently he replied, "I remember the names of people I like and are important." His frosty glare swept Campbell from head to toe. "I do remember playing this ridiculous game with you once before. Either state your business or get out of my box."

"My name is Thomas Campbell. I met you at the Grand

Hotel a few weeks ago. I also met you on a boat coming up from New Orleans about a year ago." He smiled humorlessly. "You probably have more of my money than I do. As for my business here tonight, I saw you with two lovely women and thought I might act as an escort for one of them."

Grant had begun to shake his head, but Helene interrupted, "Darling, what a wonderful idea." She turned a knowing eye to me and added, "I'm sure Althea won't mind if I get to know Thomas better. Grant," she cooed, "please let this fascinating man join us."

Grant wasn't pleased, but he nodded stiffly. "As you wish, Helene. You're our guest." As we all sat down, Grant whispered in my ear, "I think Helene has an admirer."

I nodded my head silently, but I wondered if it were true. I wasn't vain enough to think Campbell cared a whit about me. I still remembered the venomous look he'd given Grant's unguarded back that night in the dining room. I also felt uneasy that the two, Helene and Campbell, would team up. I wouldn't stand a chance.

The theater lights dimmed as the play began. I couldn't get my mind off the man behind me. It was as if his eyes were boring into my soul. I shivered. Grant leaned closer and put his strong arm around me. Feeling more protected, I settled back to enjoy the performance.

When intermission came it took me several minutes to come back to reality. It was so easy to get caught up in the imaginary hope and dreams of the actors. I heard Helene say something and when I looked around, she and Grant were gone.

"Where did they go?" I demanded of Campbell.

"Don't worry, my sweet. They just went to get us some refreshments." He leaned closer to my chair, breathing down my neck. "I'm glad they left. It'll give us time to get to know each other better."

I wasn't going to play his game. I pulled away, saying, "I

don't want to know you better. In fact, I wish you'd leave and I'd never see you again."

He chuckled softly. "Don't say that, my pet. It breaks my heart. You're so lovely. Not lovely like Helene. You have a grace that goes deeper than mere physical beauty."

I shut out his voice as he droned on and on. His compliments were as empty as his foolish head. I despised this man. I was also afraid of him. I didn't like what he was doing. Sneaking behind Grant's back, saying these things to me. What was he up to?

I felt a draft against my back. I turned, hoping to see Grant. Instead I saw a dear friend of Papa's. Gus Sawyer. With a cry of pleasure, I rushed to shake his hand. "Mr. Sawyer, how good it is to see you again."

He was a tall man. My father's age. His head of hair was fast becoming obsolete, but he was a friendly and gentle man. I'd always liked him and I knew my father trusted him. Gus' voice was deep with sorrow as he said, "It's good to see you too. My thoughts have been with you these last few weeks. I heard of William's death, but I was out of town, unable to attend the service." His eyes were steady as they looked into mine. "I heard you are married," he said, "and now at home at Willow-crest."

I nodded my head, understanding the question in his eyes. I was able to answer him honestly with Grant out of the box. "Father was a good man. I only wish he could know how happy I am. My husband is good to me. We're very content."

Gus sighed. "I'm glad to hear it. I've met your husband. He came to me for your necklace. The one made of topaz. While I was designing it, I knew it was right for you." He glanced at my throat and sighed. "I was hoping to see it on you tonight."

"I'm sorry to disappoint you, but I do adore it. You're a fine jeweler. I hope your business is doing well."

"Yes. Yes. Everything is just fine." He shuffled his feet uncomfortably. Lowering his voice, he said, "When I saw you come in, it was an opportunity I had to take, coming to speak to you. I've had something on my mind for almost a year now. With William dead, I hope you might clear it up."

I sensed what he was going to say. I answered him cautiously, "I will if I can."

Gus glanced at Campbell and raised his eyebrows in question. I followed his inquiring look. I saw the man listening with unabashed interest. I was deeply annoyed. It showed in my voice as I said, "I'd like a private word with Gus, Mr. Campbell. Would you leave us alone?"

He hesitated, but there was nothing he could do. With one last look at us, he pushed aside the curtain and stepped out into the hall. We waited until we heard his receding footsteps.

"Now," I said, "What is it?"

"I realize it isn't any of my business. The fact is, William told me to mind my own business, but I have to know." He stopped to peer into my face. "Althea, why did William have me take all the valuable gems from the Crestwood jewelry?"

I hadn't thought of Papa doing this. All this time I had pictured the whole items of jewelry. "Tell me exactly what you mean. Take them where?" I asked quietly.

"Just that, my dear. He brought all the jewelry to me and told me to remove all the stones. I was to keep the heavy settings in my safe. He put the gems in a leather pouch and took them with him. I hated to see him leave with a fortune in precious jewels, but they were his. He asked me to keep the settings for you. He said he was sure you would come to me one day."

My knees refused to hold my weight any longer. I sank into my chair. In a trembling voice, I tried to explain Papa's plan. When I finished, I asked hopefully, "He didn't give you a clue where he was going to put them?"

Gus shook his head. "I'm sorry, but he wouldn't tell me anything. You can see why I've been so worried."

I got restlessly to my feet. I was so close, yet nothing was to come of this new information. I sighed heavily with disappointment. Then my attention was caught by the gentle swaying of the curtain.

I put my finger to my lips and pointed. I started toward the back of the box. Fire was in my eye, but the curtain was pushed aside and Grant and Helene stepped in. I looked past them, meeting Campbell's eyes. I saw the naked greed in them before he pulled a veil over his true emotion. In that instant I knew he had overheard everything.

My pleasant evening was ended right then. I ignored the rest of the play. My thoughts were on the jewels and Campbell. I now knew for sure they did exist, just as Papa had said. In all my life, I'd never seen all the Crestwood jewelry massed together at one time. I saw different necklaces and brooches on Mama. The ones she didn't wear were kept locked away. Now the stones were together in a leather pouch at Willowcrest. Gus had said a fortune. If they were in a pouch, the hiding place would be quite small. It could take me forever to find them.

Later that evening, as we drove up the driveway to Willowcrest, I searched the grounds and house in my mind. The gems would be in a permanent part of the estate. I gazed about me in the bright moonlight, thinking about and rejecting any number of hiding places. I began to go over the rooms in the house again. Was there someplace I'd failed to check?

I gave an exhausted sigh as Grant lifted me easily from the carriage. I couldn't do any more about the jewels tonight, but tomorrow I would start again.

Thoughts of Papa's legacy flew out of my mind as I watched Helene thank Grant for the day. She pressed herself close, kissing him full on the lips.

"Good night, darling. Thank you for a wonderful day." With a wave of her hand, she slowly waltzed up the stairs.

I looked from her twisting skirt to find Grant's eyes still watching her. I filliped his arm harshly with my fingertips. He turned to me, a faraway look in his eyes. "I want to thank you too," I said stiffly and started to the stairs.

He took my hand and pulled me around to face him. His eyes held a playful gleam. "Aren't you going to thank me the way she did?"

I sniffed daintily, dismissing her wanton behavior with a wave of my hand. "No thank you. I've given you all the kisses you need for one day." I lowered my voice. "Besides, we're alone now. There isn't anyone to watch us carry on our act."

His voice deepened. "I've been kissed by you several times today. But I have to disagree with you on one point. It hasn't been nearly enough to suit me."

Without another word he swung me up into his arms. I must have been a load for him, but he seemed to carry me effortlessly. Upstairs he kicked our bedroom door shut and crossed to our bed, where he dumped me ungraciously. Grant stood over me, his hands on his hips. I looked up at him, wondering what was to happen next. The light of playfulness was gone from his eyes.

My dress had worked up, exposing my thighs. I pulled the dress down. It wasn't because I was feeling modest. I was confused and it was something to do. When I could look up, I found I was alone. Grant had moved away from the bed. He stood with his back to me, looking out the window. His lightning-swift change of mood was a mystery to me.

Softly I asked, "What's wrong?"

"Nothing," he said shortly. "Go to sleep."

"Are you coming too?" I almost whispered.

He turned to stare at me. It wasn't a passing glance. His blue eyes penetrated mine. A minute passed, then two. I squirmed awkwardly, wondering what was the matter. What was he thinking? Feeling? Just when I had worked up enough courage to question him, he walked out of the bedroom.

I started to call to him but couldn't. What was I to say or do to him? I wanted to follow, to comfort him, but comfort him against what? He wanted to be alone or he wouldn't have left the room. I would respect his wishes.

I got ready for bed and must have dropped right off to sleep. I awoke much later to Grant's fumbling movements and grumbling words. It was after he got in beside me that I could smell the whiskey on his breath. What had upset him? Why had he gone downstairs and gotten drunk?

The next morning Grant was dressed and gone before I woke up. I threw back the covers and hurried to dress. I wanted to see him. I wondered what his mood would be this morning. I also had to begin my search. A talk with Celia was first on my list.

Before I could leave the bedroom, Grant came back. His eyes didn't meet mine as he said, "Good morning." His voice was polite. It was like one stranger speaking to another.

I watched him, a troubled frown on my face. He took off his shirt and exchanged it for an older one. It was while he was buttoning his jacket that he explained. "I'm going to be out with the men today. John knows where I'll be. I've told him to send Jeremy for me if I'm needed." At the door he stopped to look back at me. He opened his mouth, then closed it. He was gone before I could say anything. A few minutes later, I heard the front door slam.

I felt uneasy. What had I seen in his face? Sorrow? It was as if he wanted to tell me something but hesitated. He was upset. His moods were so changeable. Did it have to do with Helene? Was he jealous of the attention Campbell had paid her last night? It hadn't seemed to bother him then. I remembered how masterful he'd been with me last night. I hadn't fought his attentions. He hadn't given me the chance. He'd just walked out and gotten drunk.

I shook my head, baffled at his actions. I knew we were both under a strain with Arthur ill and the others in the house. Maybe after spending a day outdoors with the men, Grant would come home in better spirits. I hoped so. I couldn't keep track of his different moods.

I pushed Grant to the back of my mind for the present. I went in search of Celia. I found her sitting in her room by the windows, enjoying the lovely view. I stopped outside her open door and knocked politely.

"Would you mind some company?" I asked her.

She turned with a smile. "How nice of you, my dear. Come in and have a seat."

"I don't want to bother," I said, taking the chair she indicated.

"You aren't. I'd enjoy visiting with you. We haven't had a chance to do that, have we?"

"No. Things have been rather hectic. First Arthur, then I fell." I was surprised to see her friendly eyes look away from mine, ill at ease. In a casual tone, I asked, "Do you mind if I ask you some questions?"

"What about?" she said doubtfully.

Here was my chance, but I had to be cautious. I didn't want to upset Celia. She was looking much better today. Her skin wasn't so pale and her hands lay still in her lap. I smiled warmly. "I don't want to know anything special. Just about Grant's childhood. What was he like as a little boy?"

I could see her relax. Her face brightened as she talked. "He was a fine child. He was sweet and thoughtful. Of course, I don't mean to say he didn't do daring and mischievous things. All boys are that way."

"He had a brother, didn't he? He's dead now."

Celia's smile became strained. She smoothed the dry skin on the back of her hands. "I don't like to talk about Nicholas. He's dead. Nothing I do will bring him back, though God knows I wish I could. I miss him dreadfully," she choked. "It was such a shock. A terrible tragedy. He and Helene had just been married that morning. Why that horse had to bolt and throw him,

I've never understood. His neck was broken." Her voice cracked and she closed her eyes briefly.

When she opened them, she blinked away the tears. "I don't want to talk about him, Althea. It's too upsetting. I adored Nick." Her voice was soft. "I never dreamed they would meet and fall in love. But to marry. It was a terrible mistake. I've paid for it dearly."

I didn't know what she meant and was about to question her when she added, "I should have been the one to raise Helene. Things might have been different."

I stirred in my chair. She looked at me in confusion. "Althea?" she said. "I'm sorry. I was thinking out loud. Let me explain what I meant. Helene is the daughter of one of my dearest friends. Francine is dead now. I stood by and watched Francine spoil Helene. Helene was such a beautiful child. It was easy to give in to her temper bouts. Now it isn't any wonder she still expects to get her own way. If she's denied, she doesn't give up easily."

"Why did she marry Arthur?" I asked.

Celia's face closed abruptly. Her mouth firmed into a straight line of disapproval. "That was their business. I don't intrude where it doesn't concern me." Her tone implied that I shouldn't either. Briskly she changed the subject. "What of *your* family, my dear?"

Absently I told her about Mama and Papa. I didn't concentrate on what I was saying. I didn't need to. I'd lived that life. What interested me was the life of the Whitmores.

When I finished telling of Papa's death, Celia leaned forward to pat my hand. "We're your family now, my dear. We all want you and Grant to have a happy life together."

"Not all of you want that," I said.

Celia straightened to look at me, then swiftly looked away. "What do you mean?"

"I think you know. Helene. She hasn't tried to hide her feelings for Grant."

"You must be mistaken, Althea. I know it is difficult to have your in-laws move in with you so soon after just being married. I hope you aren't feeling unsure of Grant's love. We can all see he's devoted to you. You have nothing to fear from Helene. She's a sweet child. At one time she was infatuated with Grant, but that's all done with. She looks upon Grant as a friend. A close friend. Nothing more."

I started to add what kind of a friend I thought she was but shrugged. If Celia wanted to think Helene was over Grant, far be it from me to point out she was wrong. I decided Celia only wanted to see what she wanted to.

Apparently I wasn't as good at hiding my feelings as I thought. Celia said, "I know Helene better than anyone. I watched her grow up. I continued to look after her when Francine died. She and Nicholas took me by surprise when they ran off and married. I thought I'd talked them out of such foolishness." Her voice shook, but she went on. "When she began to notice Grant, I was worried, but he had his accident and she lost interest. Helene turned to Arthur for security. I thought this a terrible thing, but I changed my mind. He was so old and she such a pretty little thing. I knew he couldn't please her like a handsome young man could, but like a silly old woman, I didn't think that would be important. I knew Arthur could give Helene anything she desired and she would live at Whitmore Halls with me. I urged them to wed." Under her breath, she sighed, "Fool that I was."

"She still cares for Grant," I repeated.

"No!" she shouted. "No! She can't!"

I heard the note of despair in Celia's voice. "But why?" I questioned softly. "Why are you against it?"

Celia swallowed nervously. "My dear, isn't it obvious? You're the woman for my nephew. He needs you at his side. And you need him too. Take care of yourself, my dear," she said. "Be careful."

"What do you mean?" I asked.

Celia closed her eyes wearily. "Please excuse me. I'm very tired. I stayed with Arthur awhile early this morning. I think I'll take a short nap before lunch." She got up and held the door open for me.

I didn't have any choice. After I had passed through, the door shut firmly behind me. Out in the hall, I stood wondering why she had warned me. Her windows faced the river. Had she seen something the day I was pushed?

CHAPTER TEN

Downstairs I found Helene in the dining room having a late breakfast. I sat down across from her and sipped a cup of tea.

"Did you sleep well?" I inquired.

She shrugged her shoulders, barely acknowledging I'd entered the room. I wanted to go find a more pleasant atmosphere, but I was curious about a few things Celia had mentioned but wouldn't elaborate on.

"I don't know anything about you," I said with a pleasant smile. "Where do you come from?"

She turned haughty brown eyes on me. "You know where I come from. Whitmore Halls."

I sighed in exasperation. "No. That isn't what I meant. Are you an only child?"

"Yes."

"Well?" I asked.

"Well what?" she asked suspiciously. "What is this all about?"

"Nothing," I said, turning away. "I just thought we might visit this morning."

Helene was silent, but the temptation to talk about herself was too great. In a minute she was telling me all about her younger life. "My mother, Francine, loved me very much. My father left her before I was born, so it has always been just the two of us. We never had much money for the things I needed. If it hadn't been for Aunt Celia, I'd never have gotten out of that mediocre existence my mother was content with."

"You've known Celia a long time?"

"Since I was born. She and Mother were old friends. Celia came to visit regularly. Then we moved to New Orleans and we saw her nearly every day." Helene turned up her nose. "She's a kindly woman. I tolerate her. She brought me beautiful dresses. She did try to meddle in the way Mother took care of me. Celia thought I was given too much freedom. When Mother died, Celia tried to make me over, but I was old enough to know what I wanted. I wanted Nicholas. When we fell in love, she was furious. Celia threatened to cut Nick off without a cent from her will. I hated that, but Nick had plenty in his own right. We ran off and got married."

"Did she ever say why she didn't want you two to marry?"

"She said with my looks I could find a man wealthier than Nick, but I loved him. At least I thought I did. It was after he died that Grant came back to Whitmore Halls." Her voice was thoughtful as she murmured, "I should have met Grant first. I'd have been his wife by now."

I ignored that and asked another question. "Did Celia know you were getting interested in Grant?"

"It wasn't easy to hide how we felt about each other," she said smugly.

Knowing how she acted in my house toward my husband, I could imagine how she acted toward Grant when they were both unattached. "What did she do?" I asked.

"She didn't *do* anything. She *said* plenty. I never *could*

understand what difference it made to her," puzzled Helene.
"Grant was her own flesh and blood. She adores him and she
loved Nick too." Helene stood up and shrugged. "It's past now.
I don't know what all these questions are about." A sneer
twisted her lips. "Are you concerned about our friendship?"
Her voice deepened dramatically on the word "friendship."
Helene laughed throatily. "Are you worried, Althea?" She
continued to laugh all the way up to her room.

I breathed a sigh of relief that she was gone. Then I left the
dining room too. I had no intention of carrying on any more
conversations with Helene. If I had any questions, I'd ask
someone else or forget them.

I walked down the front steps and crossed to a stone bench
secluded under one of the huge willow trees. Here I had the
quiet I needed to rest and think.

I wondered why Celia thought Helene too good for her
nephews. One explanation occurred to me, but I pushed it
away as being ridiculous. Before I could bring it forward again
to analyze further, I heard a horse galloping in the distance.
Thinking it might be Grant, I began walking toward the
sound. I watched the rider approach. From this distance I
couldn't see who he was, but he waved gallantly. I smiled and
waved in return until I saw who it was. My smile of welcome
faded into a dark scowl.

I didn't wait for him to dismount but stalked over to him.
"Mr. Campbell, you're trespassing on private property."

"But, my dear, I'm here at Miss Helene's kind invitation. She
said I might call on her." He bowed low, scraping his hat to the
ground.

I stared at him, trying to puzzle him out. He looked up at me
and smiled lewdly. "My dear," he purred, "should you be
staring at me like that? What if your husband is watching from
one of the windows?"

My hand itched to wipe that smug grin from his face.
Through grim lips I replied, "Did you know Helene was mar-

ried? Did you know she is only a guest here herself? Did you know her husband is a very sick man? But most important of all, did you know that I don't want you anywhere near my house?"

He threw up his hands in mock surrender. "My sweet Miss Althea. I don't know what to say first." He took a deep breath, then with exaggerated politeness counted the points on his fingers. "Yes, I know she's married. Yes, I know she's a guest here. Yes, I know he's ill. And no, I can't believe you don't want me here. You won't send me back to town without a nice cool drink first. I've ridden a long way to be with you and of course Miss Helene too."

Against my better judgment, I agreed. "Very well. Come to the house. You can visit and have your drink. Then you have to go. Understand?"

He laughed softly. "Yes, miss. Your English is perfect."

I led the way to the house and waited on the porch while he tied his horse. As Campbell entered Willowcrest, I watched his face. I saw he was very impressed. John came forward. I moved to one side to have a private word with the old butler.

"Go tell Miss Helene she has a visitor in the front parlor. Tell her it's Mr. Campbell."

I turned back to Campbell. Very ungraciously I snapped, "Come along, in here." I motioned for him to take a seat. His sharp eyes darted around the room hungrily. He saw the oil paintings, rich wall hangings and soft carpeting on the floor.

His eyes spoke his appreciation. "This is very nice. Such a tasteful room. I'd love to see the rest of the house. How about a tour later?"

I stiffened. "This is my home. It isn't open to the public. You won't see any more than this room and the hall as you leave."

"Tut, tut, child," he chided me. "What would your dear mama say, treating a guest this way?"

"Did you know her?" I demanded sharply.

"No" was his reply.

"Then don't begin to tell me what she would have thought. I suggest you leave her out of our conversation." I lowered my voice. "I don't know what you hope to accomplish here but . . ."

I stopped as Helene sauntered into the room. With a cry of delight, she cooed, "Darling. What a wonderful surprise. I had no idea I could expect you so soon. I'm glad you came. I've been so bored." She batted her long lashes at him.

I felt sick as I watched him praising Helene. When I could get a word in, I said, "I'm sure you'll both excuse me. I'll have Sarah bring you a drink, Mr. Campbell. If I don't see you again, have a pleasant trip back into town." My eyes narrowed warningly. "I'm sure you'll want to leave soon. It's such a long ride back." I nodded shortly and hurried out into the hall.

Behind me I heard Helene say. "Don't listen to her. That was a dreadful thing to say. I hope you'll stay all day."

I hurried to the kitchen, where I found John and Sarah having a cup of tea. I quickly explained there was an uninvited guest in the parlor and I didn't trust the man.

"Give him a cold drink, Sarah. If he isn't gone in an hour, come for me. I'll be in the cemetery." To John I added, "I don't want him wandering away from the parlor. If he comes out alone, I want you to follow him. Have one of the girls come for me. Don't let him out of your sight. I don't trust him," I repeated.

I left the house, knowing my orders would be carried out. I attacked the weeds that grew prolifically over the graves as if they were Campbell himself. I hadn't been at it long when I heard my name called. I was sure my hour wasn't up. I assumed he was up to no good. This thought brought me to my feet and I ran quickly to the house.

Inside all hell had broken loose. Campbell lay on the stairs, his face contorted with pain. John stood near him, glowering down at Campbell. Helene was sobbing and wringing her hands uselessly. Even Aunt Celia had come out of her room to see what was the matter. Everyone was talking at once.

I had to shout to make myself heard. "What's going on here?" They quieted only to speak in unison again. I raised my hands for silence. "Stop. John, you tell me what happened."

"I was out here in the hall watching the door, like you said, Miss Althea. I heard Mrs. Whitmore say she was going to go get her shawl. She hadn't been gone a minute when he stepped out into the hall. He looked all around, sneaky like, then went to the music room. He opened the door and looked in, then shut it. When he started for the stairs, I kept him in sight." John pointed to the sixth step. "When he got here, I stepped out of hiding and called, 'What are you doing?' That was when he fell."

Campbell moaned and tried to sit up. "You all stand there talking, but I'm in pain. Can't you get me off these stairs?"

I didn't know what to do. I *did* know he wasn't going upstairs. "Sarah, you and a couple of the girls go upstairs and get one of the folding cots. John, we'll put him in the ballroom."

"The ballroom?" shouted Helene in outrage. "But there's nothing in there."

"I know." I smiled pleasantly. "He can't climb the stairs and John and I aren't up to carrying him. In the ballroom he'll have plenty of privacy."

Helene looked undecided. Campbell looked disgusted with my plan. I directed the making up of the cot. After he was settled, I spoke to him.

"I don't know for sure why you came today. I don't know why you were snooping around my home. I do know that when my husband gets back, he'll see to it you're driven back to town. Until he comes, John will sit by your side. Be sure you stay put." I stared at him harshly. "Have I made myself clear?"

Helene drew in her breath at my tone. Campbell saw her sympathy and played for more. He turned his sad gray eyes on me. "I'm sorry. You're a hard woman, Miss Althea. You only heard your man's story. You've not given me a chance to explain."

I didn't say anything. I was tired of the sight of the man and his lies. I went into the study, but I wasn't to find peace here. Helene followed.

She glared at me. "He's right, Althea. You're treating him horribly. He's my guest. When Grant gets here, I'm sure he will see to Thomas' comfort."

My anger exploded, blotting out my good sense. Before I thought how it would sound, I said sharply. "Don't forget you're only a guest here yourself. You didn't have any business asking that man here without asking me first. If he had stayed in the parlor, none of this would have happened. But as you say, Grant will decide. However, this is my home too. I have some say in what goes on."

Celia had followed us into the study. I had my back to her and didn't know she was there. She clicked her tongue sadly. "I'm disappointed in you, Althea. I thought we were a family. Now I find you look upon us as intruders, much as that man that fell." She sighed in a hurt way and left the room.

I felt terrible. I hadn't wanted to hurt that poor woman. It didn't help to turn back and find Helene smiling maliciously. Her voice was low so she couldn't be overheard, but I heard her well.

"I knew you were jealous of Grant's attention to me, but I didn't think you were jealous of Thomas too. Or do you and he have a prior commitment? Won't Grant be happy to know of this little angle?"

"Shut up!" I shouted at her. I had let her goad me into another outburst. "I'm tired of your nasty remarks and insulting manner. I wish you'd go home. I'd like nothing better than to never set eyes on you again!"

"What's going on in here?" said a deep voice from behind me.

My harsh words echoed in my ears. Had Helene known

Grant was standing there? I looked in her triumphant eyes and knew she had. I'd done just what she wanted. I turned slowly to face my husband.

Helene didn't waste a precious second. Every word I'd said was repeated. Hearing them said by her with her intonation, I felt ashamed. But no one knew what I did. No one knew my secret. It was a secret and it would remain so. I would tell no one. The jewels were from Papa to me. I wouldn't have everyone tearing up the house looking for them. I closed my lips and listened.

When her tirade came to an end, Grant turned to me. His face was dark with anger. I waited for an explosion, but none came. He swallowed once, then asked, "What happened, Althea? When I left this morning, everything was going smoothly. I return to find a man has fallen down the stairs. John, good level-headed John, is standing guard, like the man's a criminal. I find Helene almost in hysterics. Aunt Celia passed me in the hall without a word." His voice had risen the longer he talked. Now he shouted, "I want to hear what you have to say."

I cleared my throat and looked at him coolly. "Mr. Campbell came into this house uninvited by you or me. I don't trust the man."

"But that isn't any reason to treat him so unjustly," sobbed Helene. She turned to Grant and cried, "She told me I was a guest here in her house and I didn't have any right to invite him here."

Grant turned his sharp eyes on my face. "You told her that?"

It was the truth, only Helene had left out what had taken place before I'd said it. Still, I could only nod my head. I started to tell him some of the things that had led up to my statement, but I couldn't. I was backed into a corner. I knew Grant was going to say Campbell could stay. Outside of taking him aside and telling him about the jewels and the conversation Campbell had overheard, my hands were tied. I swallowed my battered pride and tried to be gracious. The words almost gagged me.

"Perhaps I was rash. I'm sorry, Helene. I'll also apologize to Celia for my unkind words. I don't know what got into me. I shouldn't have let my personal feelings about Mr. Campbell keep you from forming a friendship with him. I'm sorry." I nodded to Helene and turned back to Grant. I could see he was bewildered by my sudden change. A moment ago I'd been fuming and now I was contrite. "I do have one condition I don't think is heartless. We don't know this man. I'd feel safer if he were to remain in the ballroom."

Helene started to object, but I held up my hand. "I think he'll be comfortable there. It's cool and quiet. Just what he needs for his recovery. It will also be easier on the servants. They have the stairs to contend with, taking things up to Arthur. I think it would be better if Campbell stays where he is."

Grant agreed. "I don't think that's unfair, Helene. We'll see he's made comfortable."

Helene didn't like the idea, but I knew I was on firmer ground. I excused myself. With grim determination, I went to the ballroom. I didn't know how I was going to get him out of the house and still keep the jewels a secret. I knew he would begin his search as soon as possible, that was his reason for coming. He didn't give a darn about Helene. His plan had been to smooth-talk me, hoping to woo me into telling him more. But I wasn't that big a fool. I had seen through his plan.

At the door I watched him, my presence unknown to him. My suspicions were confirmed about his fake accident. He lay on his back, his arms folded under his head. I heard him whistling a soft tune under his breath. "Darn him!" I swore softly.

I loathed the man. Not only had he brought me more worries, but he had driven a wedge between Grant and me. I could feel us drifting apart.

"Hello," I called. I watched in disgust as he arranged himself in a more convincing position. A mask of pain settled over his features.

"Oh," he moaned, "you'll have to come closer. I'm afraid to move my back. The pain has subsided for the time being."

"We haven't sent for a doctor. Is there a special one you would like us to call?"

"A doctor?" he repeated dumbly. "I don't want any doctor. I just need a few days' rest."

My eyes narrowed, but I kept the anger from showing. "Very well. If you need anything, just call. Someone is always nearby." I said this as a warning, then added in case he missed my subtleness, "I'd suggest you stay in your bed and rest. Getting up, roaming around my house, wouldn't be healthy."

I left before he provoked me into saying more. I knew he was laughing at me. So far he was the winner. He'd gotten his foot in the door. I knew he would be off that cot as soon as the lights were out. But I'd be waiting for him. I wouldn't sleep tonight.

Upstairs I looked at the bed Grant and I shared. Tonight I would sleep elsewhere. I knew this move would push us further apart, but it couldn't be helped. An argument would give me the excuse I needed to sleep in the sitting room off our bedroom. After everyone had settled for the night, I would sneak out the side door and go downstairs. I'd wait there on the stairs for Campbell to come out of his room. I'd give him time to get deeply involved in his search, then I'd come for Grant. We would catch Campbell in the act and Grant would toss him off Willowcrest. It was a good plan, if only Campbell would cooperate. I felt sure he would. I could still remember the greed in his eyes.

All that remained was to anger Grant. In his present mood, I didn't think that would be difficult. I took a minute to brush my hair before going downstairs to lunch. I found Grant alone at the table. He smiled a welcome. I hadn't counted on his quicksilver mood change.

"I thought I might have to eat alone. Helene insisted on lunching with her new friend and Celia is still upset." He looked at me pointedly. "I think an apology is in order."

"Yes," I sighed meekly. "I regret hurting her. That was never my intention."

"What *was* your intention?"

"I told you. I don't trust that man. He has shifty eyes."

Grant threw back his handsome head, roaring with laughter. "Shifty eyes?" he repeated. "That's all that condemns the poor man?"

"No," I muttered, my face red. "I don't like him, but apparently your stepmother finds him very attractive."

Grant stopped laughing. Sternly he said, "Why do you refer to Helene in that manner?"

"What do you mean?" I asked innocently.

"You know very well what I mean. Stepmother is hardly the way I see Helene."

I sniffed loudly. "Huh! I *bet* that isn't the way you see her!"

Grant's eyes were two tiny slits in his blazing face. "May I ask just what you mean by that remark?" he said stiffly.

"I think you know exactly what I mean."

"Do I?" he questioned coolly. "I'd rather hear it from your own lips, so there won't be any misunderstanding."

"I wouldn't dirty my mouth with the words to describe your relationship with Helene and her obvious feelings for you." I stood up, tossing my unused napkin to the table. "If you'll excuse me, I've lost my appetite."

Grant blocked my way out of the dining room. "You aren't excused. I want to know what the hell you're talking about. Helene says you're in love with Campbell and all that resentment this morning was just an act to get him in the house. Is that right?"

I looked up at him, taken completely by surprise. Suddenly I began to laugh. "Just when I think I have Helene figured out, she does something that makes me reconsider." I shook my head sadly. "If you believe that concocted story, Grant Whitmore, then you're a fool!" I ran a weary hand over my hair. "I'm tired of all this. I'm tired of seeing the loving glances Helene gives you and you do nothing to discourage. I'm tired of being a third wheel in my own house. But most of all I'm tired of the deception." I brushed past him and ran outside.

I waited for the tears to come, but I was past crying. I'd engineered this argument. I'd gone downstairs looking for these results. What I hadn't counted on was saying so many things that were close to my heart. They were words that wouldn't be easy to forget or forgive. Once Campbell was gone, could I mend things between Grant and me? Would our angry words be too much to forget?

I held my head in my hands. Was I being a fool? Was I taking too big a chance? If I went to Grant and explained everything, he'd understand my fear of Campbell. And yet there was that look I'd seen on Campbell's face that night at the Grand Hotel. I couldn't pass it off. Campbell hated Grant. Maybe it wasn't the jewels that had brought him here. Had he come to Willowcrest for another reason?

It was after meeting Campbell in the dining room that I was pushed down the embankment. What if it hadn't been Helene? Was it Campbell wishing to get rid of me, hoping to hurt Grant in this way? It was farfetched, but it was a possibility.

The afternoon passed quickly, or so it seemed to me. I was apprehensive about the coming evening. I had to tell Grant I wouldn't be sharing his bed.

At the dinner table I set things straight again with Celia. She accepted my apology graciously and I was free to excuse myself. In the bedroom I gathered my nightclothes, pillow and blanket in my arms. I almost dropped them as a voice demanded. "What do you think you're doing?"

"I'm sleeping in the sitting room," I answered him shortly.

"No!" he growled. "I forbid it!"

I whirled around, sputtering angrily. "You forbid it! You can forbid all you like, but I'm not sleeping in that bed with you. I've had all I can take of you and your family today. I just want to be left alone."

Grant took a step in my direction. I cringed from his fury. His blue eyes searched my face, then he turned away, a grim look around his mouth.

"Very well. If that's the way you want it. Sleep on that sofa. It's hard and unyielding. You deserve each other."

I kept my head high and my shoulders squared. As the door closed behind me, my shoulders slumped in dejection. An abyss had opened between us. I shut my eyes tightly, trying to shut out the pain in my heart. I loved Grant. Why couldn't it be a simple cut-and-dried love? Why were there so many problems? Nothing I'd thought or done since Grant came into my life had been simple or easy.

First he'd been the reason I'd left Willowcrest. Then he was my reason for coming home again. Such a gullible ninny I'd been to think my life would be complete just to be at Willowcrest again. I needed more than a house. I needed a home and a man to share it. Really share it. As well as sharing my bed. I needed a family to love and care for. Was I trading all hope of having those things by keeping the jewels a secret? I was my father's daughter. I was gambling, but my stakes were worth so much more than any he'd ever played with.

My thoughts and recriminations kept me occupied until the house had settled. I had opened the sitting room door that led to the hall, a fraction of an inch so I could hear when John and the others went up to their rooms.

I heard the clock chime one o'clock and knew it was time. I quietly opened the door wider and crept out into the upper hall. All the bedroom doors were closed. On silent feet, I stole down the stairs and seated myself on the next to the last step. I pressed myself next to the newel post and prayed no one would come down while I was there.

In the ballroom all was quiet. I heard Campbell move on his cot. Once he moaned rather loudly, as if in pain. Had I been wrong? Had he hurt himself? Or did he suspect I was watching over him?

I leaned my head wearily against the cool smooth wood. I was tired. It had been a long exhaustive day full of clashes and verbal abuse. Tonight I would make sure Campbell stayed in the ballroom, but what about tomorrow night? I couldn't go without my sleep indefinitely.

The hours passed slowly. Many times I wished I'd brought a pillow or had a cup of tea. But I stayed where I was, often dozing off, only to awaken with my heart beating rapidly. My dreams were full of terror and fear. Was it an omen of things to come?

Finally at five, just as the first rosy light of day was peeking in the windows, I went back to my sitting room. I closed the door softly before turning to find Helene seated on the couch. She smiled at me serenely.

"What are you doing here?" I hissed.

"I might ask you the same thing." She smiled softly. "Why aren't you sleeping with Grant. Did the two of you quarrel?"

"That isn't any of your business."

"Isn't it?" she said. Helene got up and walked over to me. "Do you think I'll sit by and let you go down to Thomas at night and not tell Grant?"

I caught my breath. I was dumbfounded by what this could do to my marriage. It hadn't occurred to me how my nightly trip downstairs would be taken. This was the ideal way for Helene to drive Grant and me further apart. Grant would never tolerate even the slightest hint of infidelity in his wife.

"I see I have made my point clear," she purred. "You can't have them both. I want Grant. He's always been mine and that simple gold band on your finger doesn't change a thing."

"Grant would never believe you," I bluffed uncertainly.

She laughed wickedly. "You don't think so? Look at you. Your hair is tousled. Your nightgown is wrinkled. You don't look like you've slept all night." She pressed her face nearer to mine. "I want Grant. Watch your step. Remember that the next time you go for a walk."

She brushed by me and was gone before I could say a word. I began to shiver. She was evil. I pulled the blanket around me, but sleep was out of the question. I sat down on the sofa, but I kept my eyes on the hall door. I would never trust my back to Helene again. At last I knew where the danger lay. Helene had all but admitted to pushing me that day down by the river. But no one had heard her. Who would they believe? Grant still looked upon my fall as an accident.

After a while I heard the house stirring to life. I couldn't begin to rest easy. I got up and dressed. I needed that cup of hot tea I'd wanted all night. Perhaps it would help soothe my nerves.

As I passed the ballroom, Thomas called to me. He was the last person I wanted to see this morning. With a sigh, I went to see what he wanted.

"What is it?" I said. "Did you sleep well?"

"I had a good night's sleep." He grinned at me and added, "You look like you could use some rest too."

"I slept fine, thank you."

His eyes narrowed. His voice was warm with sympathy. "Stairs aren't very soft are they? It was nice of you to watch over me, but next time join me. This cot isn't very wide, but it would accommodate your slim body."

"What are you talking about?" I demanded.

"Just what I said, darling. Just what I said."

His harsh laughter followed me all the way outside. I had to escape the house. Everywhere I went I found evil and hatred. He had known I was outside on the stairs. What was I to do? I had to get him out of Willowcrest. I couldn't sit up night after night. Or would I have to? Who was to decide when Campbell's back was well? It didn't look like I'd be sleeping anytime soon.

CHAPTER ELEVEN

I stayed out of everyone's way that day. My thoughts kept me company, though they were far from pleasant. That evening I'd planned to be out of the bedroom and in the sitting room before Grant came upstairs. I knew I couldn't stand another turbulent scene. I was just leaving the room when the bedroom door opened. He came to a halt, taking in my load of bedclothes.

"I see you aren't going to share my bed again tonight. May I ask why?"

I couldn't hear any anger in his voice. I looked at him, then looked quickly away. Stammering, I said, "I'd rather not say."

His blue eyes were dark. A muscle jumped in his cheek, betraying his anger, or so I thought. But I was wrong. When he spoke, all he said was "I see. I don't suppose I can change your mind?"

I turned back to him, caught unaware. I'd expected an argument and sharp words but never this hurt. It was almost my downfall. Had he spoken cruelly, I could have stormed from the room, seeking solace elsewhere. Only he wasn't being mean. He stared at me like he really did want me to change my mind.

My throat felt choked with tears, making it impossible to speak. I slowly went from the room. Haphazardly I made up my tiny bed. I lay down to wait for the chime of the clock. The sad state of my bed combined with the sorrow in my heart made me listless. I was disinterested in things around me.

As the clock struck one, I wondered if I needed to go down. I thought of that conniving man lying down there on the cot and I knew I had to go, if for no other reason than to keep him in his bed. I'd be more careful tonight. I'd already decided not to go as far down the staircase as I had last night. I would stay near the top. I would be afforded the same view, and he might not know I was near.

I put my foot on the top step, my eyes on the darkness below. Behind me I heard a sudden rush of feet. Before I could turn or protect myself, hands pressed at my back. With a scream of terror, I pitched headlong down the stairs. I thought I'd never come to a stop. When I did come to a rolling halt, I lay still, afraid to move. I could hear footsteps above me. I wondered if they belonged to my killer or my savior. Off to one side, I heard Campbell shouting for help. He remained on his cot. I smiled dizzily. He couldn't give up his act for a minute, even to come see if I was dead.

It was Grant who reached me first. He checked my arms and legs for broken bones, then he began to growl and snap at me. "What in the hell were you doing? Are you in pain?"

"I'm all right. Just dizzy from rolling down all those stairs."

He picked me up in his arms and carried me back up to our room. As we passed Celia, she patted my arm with a trembling hand. "Poor dear," she murmured. Her face was ashen—from concern for me or was it something else?

Helene stepped forward. Her eyes were knowing, but her voice was innocent. "Althea, where were you going at this time of night?"

I ignored her and hoped Grant would do the same. I was in no mood to go into my trips downstairs to watch Campbell. Another attempt had just been made on my life.

He laid me on the bed. "Do you need a doctor?"

I slowly shook my head. I swallowed my rising hysteria. I was frightened. "I want Hilda," I said. I put a trembling hand to my mouth. I repeated louder. "I want a friend in this house!" I heard the shrillness in my voice, but I was past caring. "I want Hilda here tonight. Have Raymond go for her. I can't bear being alone anymore." I beat at the bed with clenched fists. "I can't stand this! I won't rest until she's here at the side of this bed!"

"God, Althea. What's gotten into you?" gasped Grant.

I didn't speak but glared up at him stubbornly.

Grant threw up his hands in defeat. "All right. If that's what you want, but I swear I don't understand any of this. You aren't alone. Why do you say you haven't any friends here?" When I still didn't answer, he tried another tack.

"You realize it's after one in the morning?"

"Hilda won't care and neither do I."

Grant looked at me for another minute, then walked to the door. I suppose everyone had gathered for news of me. Grant explained, "She's all right. I think she'll be sore in the morning. You all go on back to bed. Raymond," he called. "Go to town and get Hilda. Have her pack some extra clothes. She'll be staying for a few days." He shut the door and came back to look down at me. "All right?" he asked.

"Thank you," I said. I was getting more control of my fears, now that I knew help was coming. I looked up at him. "Grant," I said. "Someone pushed me. They hit me in the back the same way it happened down by the river." I knew better than to expect sympathy, but I hardly expected to be reprimanded so ruthlessly.

"If you'd stayed in your own bed, none of this would have happened," he snapped coldly. "I don't know what you find so irresistible about that man Campbell! But it has to stop. I won't have my wife playing the harlot in my own home." He strode around the room. "That's bad enough, but now that you've been caught, you haven't the decency to be truthful. Nothing but more lies!" His voice was bitter. "Why don't you admit it, Althea? You were on your way to meet your lover and tripped in your haste!"

"I won't admit it because it isn't true," I cried to him. "He isn't my lover now, nor has he ever been my lover. I hate the man. I didn't slip on the stairs. I was pushed."

Grant jerked aside the curtains to peer out into the darkness. When he turned back to me, his temper was barely under control. "Why do you feel you're in danger? This is the second time you've said you were pushed. Tell me, Althea," he smirked nastily, "who do you think wants to be rid of you? Me? Or is it my father? Do you think he's faking his paralysis?"

"That's a terrible thing to say to me," I began, but Grant interrupted me.

"I think it's terrible for you to say one of us wants to harm you." We glared at each other. Grant broke our strained silence. "All right," he said, running his fingers through his ruffled hair. "Suppose I believe you. Let's say you were pushed. By who? Who knew you would be going downstairs tonight?" Before I could say anything, he added softly, "Besides me."

I forgot about Helene. I asked, "Besides you?"

"I know this is your second trip to him. I heard you go down last night."

This was taking me by surprise. Playing for time so I could gather together my thoughts, I repeated dumbly, "Second trip?"

Grant frowned at me in disgust. "Don't act the fool, Althea. I know better. Last night you were gone for more than five hours. Why did you marry me, if you cared for another? Was it for the house? William told me how much you love Willowcrest."

I couldn't answer him. I lay back against the pillows, sick in body and soul. All Grant's angry words and accusations whirled through my tired and weary mind. I could understand how he had gotten the wrong impression. But what was I to do? I longed to see Hilda. I needed her shoulder to pour out my troubles on.

Even though I knew Grant was furious with me, I felt protected with him in the room. I felt my resistance slip away and I drifted off to sleep.

I woke up to the soft murmur of voices. Tears of relief filled my eyes at the sight of Hilda. All I could do was open my arms to her. Over her shoulder, I saw Grant watching us. I tried to keep my voice casual as I said, "I want to speak to Hilda alone. Why don't you sleep downstairs in the study? That way our talking won't disturb you. When I'm ready to go to sleep, Hilda can stay here with me."

"You have it all arranged, don't you?" He picked up his pillow from his side of the bed. Nodding his head to Hilda, he spoke to me. "As you wish, my dear." He left the room.

I knew I was hurting him deeply, but I forced myself not to think of him. I had to worry about myself too. When the door had closed behind Grant, I turned to Hilda. Now that she was at my side, I didn't know where to begin.

"Thank you for coming," I said, clasping her hand. I gestured to the mirror across the room. "I look in need of some help, don't I?" I tried to laugh, but it came out a weak croak. My lips were bruised and puffy. One eye was almost swollen shut. What was really painful were the parts that didn't show. My ribs and shoulders ached. I had a grazed place on one elbow.

"What happened, Althea?" she asked. Hilda had gotten a bowl of cool water and was bathing my face.

I relaxed and began my story. I told it all. When I'd finished, Hilda had an amazed look on her face. She was silent for a while, digesting it all.

"You still don't know where the jewels are?" she asked.

"No. I don't have a clue. I have to find them and put them in a safe place where people like Campbell can't find them.

Grant thinks I'm sneaking down at night to be with Campbell. The truth is I can't leave him alone. I spent the night before on the stairs and planned to do the same tonight. That was where I was going when I was pushed."

"Did you see who it was?"

"No. I didn't have to. I know it was Helene. She wants Grant." I held out my hands. "What am I to do, Hilda? I don't trust that woman."

"I don't know," she murmured truthfully. "You have a man downstairs who knows about a fortune in jewels hidden here. He could be a murderer, Althea. I think we should concentrate on him first. After he's gone, you can deal with Helene."

"But how do we expose him without telling everyone about the jewels?" I demanded. "Campbell isn't a fool." I grinned suddenly. "At least I know he won't be searching the house tonight. Grant is in the study."

"That's well and good for tonight but what about later? You can't go down every night and sit on the stairs. You also know Grant won't be content to stay out of his bedroom for very long." A frown creased Hilda's kind face. Her eyes narrowed. "Is that why you wanted me to come? To help guard him?"

I nodded reluctantly. "Partly. I do need the help, but I also need a friend. I'm scared, Hilda. I don't know what to do. Grant doesn't believe me when I say I'm in danger. I'm so sore and tired from last night that I feel that Campbell could steal the entire house and I wouldn't know the difference."

I yawned widely and sighed, "I'm so tired. You think about what I've said. Tell me your decision in the morning." Knowing Hilda was within calling distance and Grant was inadvertently guarding Campbell, I fell into a deep dreamless sleep.

Making up for lack of sleep the last few nights, I slept off and on all day. It was late afternoon when I woke up to find Hilda at my side, a cup of hot tea ready.

I sighed with appreciation as I took a sip. "That's just what I needed." I watched her as I drank my tea. When I set the cup and saucer back on the nightstand, I said, "Well? What have you decided?"

She cleared her throat, looking uncomfortable. "I've been thinking, Althea. I don't know what to do. You know I'd do anything for you, but this is dangerous. I don't like it and I don't like the position you are in."

I leaned back in dejection. If Hilda left, I didn't know what I could do. She was my only hope.

Hilda watched me and frowned. "I visited with Helene today. She asked after you and seemed genuinely concerned for your well-being. She's been very kind to me too. I ate lunch with her and Grant. Helene was polite and friendly toward Grant, but she seemed more like an old friend. Not his lover. And Grant barely noticed her." Hilda shook her head. "Althea, could you be wrong about her interest in Grant?"

In my mind I went over all the conversations I'd heard and touching scenes I'd witnessed. Slowly I nodded my head. "I'm sure, Hilda. She told me she wants Grant. She also said for me to watch my step when out walking."

"All right," agreed Hilda. "I've asked Grant if he would mind staying in the study another night. I explained that you were still upset. He wasn't pleased." Hilda laughed. "Actually he was furious, but he didn't say anything."

"Thank you for that. I don't think I could bear sleeping with him until I get this all cleared up."

"You have two things to straighten out as far as I can see," said Hilda.

"I know. Do you have any ideas about Campbell?"

"Only one," she said stoutly. Hilda folded her arms rigidly across her chest. "The truth seems to be your best action."

I started to argue, but she overrode my objection. "I say the truth is best, but I won't press you, my dear. I'll do what *you* think is best."

"Oh, Hilda," I sighed, "thank you." I was relieved. Now I knew she would help me. I closed my eyes.

Morning sunshine streamed in the bedroom windows the next time I opened my eyes. The sheer panel curtains stirred lazily in the fresh morning breeze. Carefully I stretched my legs and was relieved to find them less painful. I got out of bed slowly and belted my robe around me. I moved to the mirror for a closer inspection.

I gingerly touched my split lip and swollen eye. Hilda had pulled my long hair straight back in an unattractive braid. It hung, limp and unappealing, down the middle of my back. This did nothing to improve my sorry looks.

When the bedroom door opened to admit Grant, I turned away, too embarrassed to let him see me. He did nothing to ease my discomfort.

"You look terrible," he said with a shake of his head. "I hope you don't feel as bad as you look."

I tried to hide the hurt in my eyes. My voice was expressionless as I said, "Thank you. You've made me feel much better."

He chuckled and came to stand by me. "I'm sorry, Althea. I hope you are better. You gave us all a scare." Under his breath, he added, "I hope you learned your lesson."

I bristled, "What is that supposed to mean?"

He replied sarcastically, "Don't go downstairs without a lamp to guide you."

"That isn't funny," I said. "I told you what happened."

"I don't want to discuss it," he snapped at me. "I'm not in the mood to discuss anything having to do with your lover!"

"He's not my lover!" I shouted at him. "Don't you dare say that again! I wish you would just forget about him."

"That's easy enough to say, but tell me how to do it. He's here under my nose. I wish his back would get better. I want him gone!"

"I do too. If you'll remember, I was the one who didn't want him to stay. He's a friend of your step—" I stopped and started again. "He's a friend of Helene's. I was told to be nice to him."

"Don't be too nice!" growled Grant. Seeing I was about to

explode again, he added, "I'm leaving the house so I'll not be tempted to punch him in the mouth." He grinned at me. "Helene and I are going into town."

If he saw a tinge of green jealousy around my mouth, he chose to ignore it. "She has some things she wants to get. I've promised to take her to the theater while we're in town." His lips twisted into a smile of malice. "I'm sorry you don't feel well enough to join us. I guess that will have to be your punishment for straying." He gave me a mocking bow before slamming the bedroom door behind him.

I was left to fume in private. I was furious with him and with Helene. She wanted to be alone with Grant. Lord only knew what lies she would tell him.

"Darn them both!" I muttered to myself. "I don't care what they do." I said this out loud, but inside I knew it was a lie.

Two big tears rolled down my cheek. If Grant decided he wanted Helene, I wouldn't stand in his way. I needed those jewels more than ever. I had to put my mind to work. Over and over I tried to think of places I could look. When Hilda came with my lunch tray, I got her to help me remember the past. To my surprise, she had already been reminiscing.

"I thought of one place," she said. "Have you checked inside the piano? Or in the study? You and William used to spend hours in there."

"I've searched everywhere, using the excuse of spring cleaning. However, Grant was always in the study. Your idea of the piano is wonderful. I never thought of it. Go now!" I urged her. "I can't wait for you to go check."

I forgot about my lunch as I waited for Hilda to come back. One look at her face told me the pouch hadn't been there. I felt a wave of disappointment wash over me. I pushed it aside. It would have been too good to be true to have found it so easily.

Instead I had Hilda help me dress. I wasn't going to spend the day in bed. The dress was a simple cotton, the color of spring leaves. It looked well with my auburn hair but clashed terribly with my new blue bruises. This thought caused me to chuckle. My amusement ended quickly as Grant stormed into the room.

Hilda took one look at his face and quietly excused herself, leaving us alone.

"You must be feeling better," he said. "Are you thinking of accompanying us to town?"

I turned my back to him, picking up my hairbrush. My eyes met his in the mirror. "Do you think it would be wise to be seen publicly with a face like this?"

"Does it matter to you what people think?"

I knew he was referring to my supposedly torrid romance with Campbell. I ignored that and smiled brightly, trying to hide my pain.

"Apparently it doesn't matter to *you.* You're escorting another woman to dinner and the theater. Don't you think that might cause talk?"

Grant raised an eyebrow. "Are you jealous, Althea?"

I spoke through stiff lips. "Why should I be jealous?"

Grant chuckled, coming to stand behind me. A finger gently traced a delicate pattern on my bare arm. "I don't want you to be sad. If you're jealous, just say so. I'll send someone else with Helene."

"Huh!" I muttered. "Why should you do that? Isn't this a wonderful opportunity for you? You won't have to worry about my prying eyes."

Grant's eyes narrowed. His hand dropped away from my arm. "You're a sly cat, Althea. Your claws are sharp. What I do I do in front of you. I don't sneak down the stairs in the dead of night to meet my lover."

I was speechless at his lashing out at me, but he wasn't finished. "Just to set your mind at ease, Aunt Celia will be going with us. She hasn't been out of this house since she arrived. I'm sure she's in need of a change of scenery."

I watched him walk out the door. I ached to call to him. To tell him I was sorry and that I loved him. I felt humiliated and ashamed of all I'd said. Why couldn't I hold my tongue when around him?

I needed to escape this room. It suddenly felt like a prison as the four walls started to close in around me. I ran to the door and walked out onto the balcony. I was unprepared for the terror that engulfed me.

I remembered my feeling of helplessness as I rolled down the stairs. It would take some time for me to forget. I was so lost in thought I didn't know anyone was near me until I felt a hand on my arm.

I threw up my hands in a gesture of defense. When I saw it was only Celia, I slowly lowered them and tried to smile.

"My dear," she said. "I didn't mean to frighten you. I just wanted to ask if you were better." Her kind eyes traveled over my face. She clicked her tongue in sympathy. "You poor child. What a terrible thing to happen. I'm so glad it wasn't serious. Your bruises will heal. Thank the Lord."

I smiled shakily. "You startled me. I was on my way to see Arthur. I haven't been in for some time. Is he improved?"

She sighed deeply. "No, my dear. He's the same. I feel so helpless. I'm used to him being gruff and outspoken. Now all he can do is lie there and make that dreadful sound in his chest." Her face brightened somewhat as she added, "Grant's taking me for an outing. Helene has some things to get and I thought I'd better go along. She can't go with Grant by herself."

I tried to read her face, but she turned away, saying, "It wouldn't look right. Grant's a happily married man. I trust him, just as you do, my dear, but it might cause unnecessary talk." Before I could say anything, she hurried back to her room.

I stared after her. Celia said she trusted Grant, but she hadn't mentioned any trust in Helene. Had Celia changed her mind about Helene's feelings toward Grant? Did she suspect the accidents I'd been having weren't accidents at all?

I knew she liked and approved of me. Surely she wouldn't let anything happen to me if she could prevent it. This thought should have eased my mind, but it didn't. I knew how she adored Helene. Celia loved her friend's spoiled daughter. But did she love her enough to protect her from my suspicions?

There in the bright warm hallway, I shivered. I hurried around the balcony to Arthur's room.

CHAPTER TWELVE

I lounged in the study, forgotten by the excited group in the hall. They left the house, but Helene's bright high-pitched laughter remained, touching my spine like icy fingers, chilling me. I was mixed up. I felt glad to have them gone. For a few hours, I was assured there would be no quarrels between Grant and me. But I didn't like the idea of his being so long in the company of Helene. Even with Aunt Celia along, I was worried. The young woman was devious. Celia, of her own volition, admitted Helene was spoiled and used to getting her own way. What would Helene do today? Grant was already unsure of me. He suspected me of the worst possible thing a wife could do to her husband. Adultery. Just the word sounded dirty, and Grant was applying it to me.

Now with them gone, the afternoon and evening stretched out before me. I glanced at the shelves of books on the surrounding walls. From where I lay, different titles brought back good memories. Papa had liked me to read aloud. We spent many hours here before the fire.

This thought reminded me of the jewels. I wondered what Campbell was thinking. I got up slowly and made my way to the ballroom. He lay on his side, staring out into space.

"Hello," I said.

He turned to look at me. "Well, well. I wondered how you were. Helene said you were fine, but I didn't know if I could believe her."

His words left me wondering what he and Helene talked about when they were alone. I stared at him thoughtfully. He met my eyes innocently. I finally asked, "How are you?"

"I'm some better. I'm being cared for, but I do lack for company."

I shrugged my shoulders. "I'm all there is this evening. Everyone's gone except me, Hilda and the servants." After I'd said that, I wanted to bite off my tongue. Fool! I berated myself. I'd been so unhappy with my thoughts, Campbell had caught me off guard.

I smiled quickly. "They'll be back soon."

Campbell moved on the cot. "I heard all the excitement in the hall. When will they be back?"

"Soon," I repeated. "They only went to visit a sick neighbor. To deliver a pot of soup Agnes prepared." I knew I was stammering and my fast speech was giving me away, but still I chattered on. "Soup is good for you and Agnes makes some of the best." I started to back toward the ballroom door. "I think I'll go watch for them."

Campbell swung his feet off the cot. I cleared my throat. "What are you doing?" I demanded, but I heard the nervousness in my voice.

Campbell chuckled merrily. "You're not a good liar, Althea." He put a hand down to his foot and pulled out a knife.

It was then I noticed for the first time he had his boots on in bed. My eyes stayed on the knife, but I hissed, "You knew they were going all along?"

He chuckled again. "Of course. Helene came to tell me good-bye." Swiftly he crossed to my side, pressing the point of the knife to my throat. "Keep quiet or I'll kill you." He shook his head mockingly. "You must take me for a fool. Did you really think I would believe all that gibberish about soup to neighbors? Helene said not to expect her back until midnight. That should give us plenty of time to search."

Campbell jerked me around, twisting my arm behind my back. "Come on. We're going to the kitchen."

He had everything thought out. We found the help in the kitchen either eating or finishing up. Because he held a knife to my throat, it was easy to persuade them into an upstairs bedroom, where the door was locked. Campbell pushed me to one side and took Hilda as hostage. Gone was his smooth tongue. His gray eyes glittered dangerously. I was reminded of Hilda's words. Campbell could be a murderer. Now I was sure she had spoken the truth.

"I know you care for this woman or you wouldn't have sent for her at one o'clock the other night. Do as I say or I'll kill her."

I nodded my head, gulping away my fear. "Please let me talk to the nurse in Arthur's room." He waved the knife warningly but agreed. I spoke briefly through the door, explaining the situation. "Just stay in the bedroom and everything will be fine." I said.

"Smart woman," smirked Campbell.

"Now what?" I asked. My eyes strayed to the knife in his hand. "Please. Take that knife away from Hilda's throat. I'll do as you say. If you should fall or trip, you'd kill her."

"That's a thought," he said uncaringly. "Where's John?"

"John?" I repeated blankly. But I knew what he meant. John hadn't been in the kitchen with the others. For a brief moment, I prayed he'd heard what was happening and had gone for help.

We started back downstairs. I went ahead, leaving Campbell to follow with Hilda. I was glad to see he'd put the knife away for the time being.

Once downstairs, I turned to Campbell to see what he planned to do next. He was just about to reach for Hilda again when a roar of rage echoed around us.

I turned to see John charge Campbell. Since the villain was taken unaware, they both tumbled to the floor. John, the element of surprise on his side, landed a hefty punch to Campbell's nose. The blood gushed.

Campbell scrambled up, swiping at his nose with his hand. "Old man," he grunted. "I've had enough out of you!" He reached for his knife and stabbed John once in the chest.

John's eyes registered surprise. His face slowly relaxed as he slumped to the floor. Bright red blood spread out in a puddle around him. His old body twitched, then he lay still.

Hilda screamed. I felt faint. Upstairs the servants began to beat on the doors. It sounded like the whole house was going to come crashing down around us.

Campbell silenced Hilda with a backhand across her mouth. He shouted to the others to stop or he would kill me. They must have heard him above the noise, because soon they gradually quieted. I tried not to look at John's body, but my eyes were drawn to him. It was a cruel hand crushing my arm that pulled me back. I turned to glare at Campbell.

"Why did you kill him? He was just an old man."

"That might be true, but he was far from harmless," snapped Campbell, using his handkerchief to wipe his nose again. "Now I'll know where the old man is and you know I mean business."

"I never doubted it," I declared hotly. "I knew all along what you wanted. My only regret is not telling Grant. He would have gotten rid of you in no time!"

His only answer was to twist my arm tighter. "Shut up. I want those jewels."

"You heard me say Papa hid them. I don't know where they are. I've looked upstairs and in most of the rooms down here. I can't find them."

He flung me away in disgust. "I don't want any trouble from either of you. We're going to find those gems if I have to kill both of you, and I have the means to do it." He used his handkerchief to wipe John's blood from the blade of his knife. "I've killed before. I'll do it again. I need those jewels and I aim to have them. Thanks to your husband, I have next to nothing. When I overheard your conversation, I knew it was the answer to my problems. I'd get the jewels and make Grant Whitmore pay for what he did to me."

"You didn't have to gamble with Grant!" I pointed out.

He shrugged. "Maybe not, but he could have given me another chance to win back my losses. Him and his self-righteous nose stuck in the air, like he was smelling something bad when I came around. Now I have a chance to even the score." His laughter ran through the house like water off a flat rock. He jeered at me, "I'd love to see your husband's face when he comes home. I plan on having a wonderful surprise waiting for him."

"What?" I demanded.

"It would give me great pleasure to kill you, my dear. I have watched you mock me and ridicule me, but before you've breathed your last, you and I will have some fun together. I'm looking forward to seeing what you have hidden under those petticoats."

His eyes ran hungrily over my breasts and I held my breath. I didn't bother to deny or challenge anything he said. I just waited, praying his greed was strong. It was.

"We have about eight hours to find those stones. We'll take one room at a time. Since I've already searched the ballroom, we'll begin in the kitchen."

I started to say there wasn't any need. Papa and I had never shared any happy moments in there. We had Agnes to do the cooking. But I let him herd us that way. It was a way to pass away the time. Grant might return early, if I was able to prolong Campbell's discovery. I also felt a ray of hope as I watched Campbell put away his knife. I glanced at Hilda and saw her eyes were on his action too. Unfortunately Campbell noticed us watching him.

"Don't get foolish, ladies," he cautioned us. "This is my favorite weapon." He pulled the knife out again, holding it balanced in the palm of his hand. "Isn't it something?"

Against our will, our eyes were drawn to its wicked beauty. The knife was a work of art. It had a long dangerous blade, razor-sharp, and curving tip. The handle was made of polished green jade with streaks of black and white.

"I won it in a game of cards," boasted Campbell. "Just so you won't think I'm completely unarmed without it, take a good long look at this. I won *it* too." He pulled a gun from his pocket. "I don't normally use a gun, but sometimes it's more effective than a knife." He cradled the gun in his hand. "Don't let the size fool you. It's deadly." The gun was about eight inches long. Its silver and mother-of-pearl handle gleamed in the sunlight. He checked it to see if it was loaded. "The bullets are small but adequate. It isn't as quiet as a knife but quicker sometimes."

"My father always said it was a coward who stood behind a gun or a knife," I said with my nose in the air.

Campbell laughed. "Frankly I don't care what you think of me. All I want is the jewels and to get the hell out of here." He motioned toward the kitchen door. "Get in there. We're wasting time. Just remember I have both the knife and the gun. I mean business."

The kitchen smelled of roasting meat. I looked around at all the cabinets and large storage bins. He pointed the gun at me and growled, "Don't just stand there! Get busy!"

I opened a couple of cabinet doors and peeked in. I felt his eyes on me. His voice was quiet as he asked, "Is that the way you search for something?"

"I don't know where to look," I admitted.

"Do it this way," he bellowed with a loud obnoxious laugh. He walked over to one of the bins. He kicked at it savagely, pushing it over. Flour spilled out on the floor. Using the toe of his boot, he shuffled it around. "Now this is the way you look for something. Get at it. I want everything dumped on the floor."

"But this is silly," I cried. "I know they aren't in here. It's just a waste of good supplies and time."

"Come on, woman. I don't want any back talk from you. Your father is dead. How do you know where he hid the jewels? If he was fool enough to hide them, who knows where the old man put them." He shoved me to my knees and put the cocked gun to my head. "You either help me or we end it here and now."

I stared up at him, then slowly began to paw through the flour. We worked, but only halfheartedly. It was horrible, this mess we were creating. Campbell watched Hilda and me until he was sure of our willingness to work, then he began to search on his own. He didn't mind what he broke or spilled. He dumped pots of flowers off the windowsills. He pushed canned fruit and vegetables off the shelves.

I spoke bitterly, "You don't honestly believe you'll find the pouch in one of those pots, do you?"

He swung around. "Shut up!" he shouted hoarsely. "If you worked your hands and mind as fast as you worked that smart mouth of yours, we'd be done by now."

I closed my lips, but I watched him wryly. At this rate he would destroy Willowcrest. I now knew this was the surprise he had planned for Grant's homecoming. This and of course my death.

An hour later, I was sure this was his plan. My eyes wearily surveyed the ruin. Flour, sugar, tea and coffee lay on the floor. These had been tracked all over the kitchen floor. Dishes lay broken and the glass crunched underfoot.

Campbell looked around the room, a pleased expression on his face. "Very well done, ladies."

"Grant will hunt you down and I'll be at his side," I spoke fiercely.

Campbell only pointed the gun at me and waved us into the dining room. My heart nearly broke at the sight of this destruction. Anger and frustration drove him mad as he tossed things around. A silver tea service flew out the window, shattering glass everywhere. He even made us roll up the dining room rug so he could gouge and dig at the oaken floors, trying to find a loose board. Finding none, he went to the china cabinet. I bit my lip as I watched him attack Mama's fine dishes. When I could stand it no longer, I cried, "Why do you do this? Those dishes were my mother's. Please stop!" I begged. "Don't break any more."

A nasty grin spread slowly across his face. "My, my. This is quite the change from the hellcat of before." He put down the dish he'd been holding in order to swagger over to me. He leaned close. "What'll you give me to stop?"

I glanced uneasily at Hilda. "I don't have anything to give."

He laughed lewdly. "You have plenty to give, sweetheart. I'll settle for a kiss right now. But it can't be just a peck on the cheek. I want a real friendly kiss." He waved his gun at Hilda. "You get back up against that wall. There's a bargain to fulfill." He leered down at me. "If you try anything, I'll blow her head off. Understand?"

I nodded slowly. "If I kiss you, you'll stop breaking those dishes?"

"Of course I will. You have my word on it." He put his arm around my waist and pulled me up next to him. He glanced once more to Hilda before his lips came down on mine. I willed myself to be strong, but I could feel the bile welling up in my throat. I knew if he didn't stop, I'd be sick all over him and me.

When his hand began to caress my breast, I broke away to glare at him indignantly. "That wasn't part of the bargain. I've given you my kiss. Let's go on to another room."

He stepped back, his eyes on my heaving bosom. "Next time you ask a favor, be prepared to give more than a kiss." He herded us out the door but in passing gave the cabinet one last kick. Three more dishes rolled out and crashed to the floor.

I whirled at the sound. I looked at the broken pieces, then back at Campbell's grinning face. I shook my head in disgust. "So your word isn't worth anything either. I might have known. Papa was always right."

He grabbed a handful of my hair. Jerking me back, he shouted, "I'm glad your father is dead, little lady. If he wasn't, he soon would be. I'm sick and tired of hearing about him. Understand?"

I stared up at him, furious. "You wouldn't have liked him at all. William Crestwood was an honest man."

"Shut up!" he bellowed, thrusting me away. "Let's get into the room with the piano."

In here Hilda and I searched more carefully. This was the one room I thought we might be lucky. Campbell thought so too. He didn't rush about in his usual haste but took one wall at a time, dividing his attention between us and the articles he was looking at.

I began to breathe easier. I didn't want him ransacking my home. Since he had both a gun and a knife, I didn't have any choice. I cursed myself for underestimating his nature. I had never dreamed he would kill. I had guessed that he was a petty thief. Nothing more. He had killed John and we weren't out of danger either.

I glanced at Campbell and was filled with a staggering hatred and loathing. I would make him pay for John's death and the humiliation he was heaping on Hilda and me. I was smart enough to know now wasn't the time for revenge. But I would watch and wait and when the opportunity presented itself, I would strike. It was him or us. I would be ready.

I jumped as a vase slammed to the floor. I turned to him. He pulled the knife from his boot and waved it threateningly.

"Where are they? Your old man must have told you something!" He had a wicked gleam in his eye as he began to twist his wrist, making the knife blade move in a tight circle. "What did he tell you, Althea?"

I struggled to keep my fear from showing. "He wanted me to find the jewels but not right away. He used the jewels as bait for me to marry Grant. I've searched the house before. I'm beginning to think they really don't exist."

"Don't lie to me! Remember, I was there when that old man came to you at the theater. I heard him with my own ears telling you about that fortune your father took away in the leather pouch."

"Papa might have sold them to pay off some debts," I started to say, but Campbell lost control. He brought his hand around. I saw it coming, but I was too slow. It connected with a loud pop to the side of my head. I tasted blood on my tongue. My ears rang. I didn't utter a sound, but I heard Hilda's sharp gasp. I wiped my lip with the tail of my dress.

"That's just a sampling of what I'll give if you don't get busy. I want those jewels! I'm not a fool. Now unless you want to see what else I can do, let's move on. Time is wasting away."

The parlor was treated like the kitchen. It was all so uncalled for. Papa and I never came in here. This room was reserved for callers we either had not expected or didn't know. Old friends were ushered into the study or the music room. I was sure the jewels weren't in here. To forestall any scenes, I went to the fireplace and began to test for loose bricks. Apparently this suited Campbell. He left me alone.

I was lost in thought, only coming back to the present when I heard the sound of ripping cloth. I turned and saw Campbell using his sharp knife to rip open the chairs and sofa. He was like an animal. All the beautiful velvet and satin covers were being slashed beyond repair. He saw me watching and pointed to the stuffing.

"Get down there and look through that stuff. Your old man might have had one of these chairs redone."

I started to shake my head no but stopped. What good would it do? He didn't believe anything I said. While Hilda and I searched through the stuffing, Campbell threw pictures off the walls. Once in a while, he would tap gently on the wall, trying to hear if there might be a secret hiding place. After an hour of searching and destruction, he gave up.

"Where can they be?" he said softly. He turned to me and exploded, "If I find out you've been lying to me . . . I'll kill you, but first I'll let you watch me torture your friend here." He gestured toward Hilda.

"No!" I cried. "Leave her alone. I'm not lying. I just don't know where Papa put them."

Campbell continued to stare at me, and I added with an honest tilt of my chin, "I'd get them in an instant if it would mean you would leave. I never want to set eyes on you again."

He nodded his head. "I feel the same way about you. I hate the sight of you. But I do think you're telling the truth about the jewels. Let's go," he ordered.

We left the wreckage of the parlor to go to the study. I trembled at the havoc he would bring to this, my favorite room. As we walked in the door, the first thing he spotted was Grant's liquor cabinet. He smiled his appreciation. "Ah, yes. Just what I need. A good stiff drink."

Campbell picked up a full bottle and took a long swig. He wiped his lips with the back of his hand. Giving a gross belch, he sighed, "Very good whiskey, but then Grant *does* have excellent taste."

I felt a shiver of fear. If he started to drink, he would become more belligerent than ever. I looked at Hilda and saw she was having the same thought. I prayed he would drink himself into a drunken stupor but didn't think we would be that lucky. Before he passed out, I was sure he'd do as much damage as he could. I only hoped Hilda and I could stay out of his way.

With Campbell discouraged and drinking heavily, my fears were confirmed. The room was fast becoming a shambles. His first act was to pull down a whole case full of books. In the fast fading daylight, the dust rose like a cloud. Without regard to the damage he was doing, he stomped across the books, tearing out pages and bending the bindings. He went to the desk and began to pull out drawers. If one stuck or was locked, he used his knife ruthlessly to get it open.

I felt sick to my stomach at the sound of splintering wood. When he split the leather of Papa's chair, I took a step forward. Hilda held my arm.

In a whisper, she warned me. "No, Althea. Last time all he demanded was a kiss. He said he'd want more the next time. It isn't worth it. Grant can replace and mend everything that's been broken. But if this fool harms you, there won't be anything Grant can do. Let him be!"

I knew Hilda was right, but it hurt to see all the things I loved and had held precious being destroyed. My lips trembled as I smiled my thanks to Hilda. I quietly went over to a shelf of books. At random I pulled out one or two, pretending to check the pages. For what? I laughed to myself. It seemed a silly thing to do, but it kept me busy and my mind off Campbell.

I noticed he'd laid the gun on the corner of the desk. I turned my eyes away from it. I'd seen what he could do with a knife. I had no intention of finding out what he could do with a gun.

I pulled out another book. Glancing at the title, I felt tears fill my eyes. This was one of Papa's favorite stories. Noticing one of the pages had come loose, I pulled it out, intending to fold it and later repair it when this nightmare was over. Instead of a page from the book, I recognized Papa's handwriting and a sketch of the headstone.

"What's this?" I muttered to myself.

Campbell heard me and crossed the room in a leap. "What did you find?" he demanded eagerly.

I was puzzled and handed him the paper. We both studied it. He had forgotten about Hilda. Suddenly he whirled around. She had been by the windows, but now she was silently edging toward the gun on the desk.

With an evil leer, he quickly picked it up. "Is this what you were after?" He pointed the gun at her and fired.

Hilda and I both jumped in fright at the sound of the shot. The smell of gunpowder was sickening. His cynical laugh filled the air. "Next time I won't miss. Get over there to the sofa and sit there! This paper could be it!"

Hilda did as directed. My heart went out to her. She was so scared that she was trembling. I was too. My heart had nearly stopped when the gun was pointed in her direction.

"What's this?" said Campbell, gesturing at the paper.

I turned to him reluctantly. My voice quivered as I explained, "It's a drawing of the headstone that marks Papa's grave. He had the stone specially made and shipped up here from New Orleans." I pointed to a small square drawn near the bottom of the stone. "What's that supposed to mean? There isn't any such thing on the stone."

Campbell's eyes were bright. He pulled the knife from his boot and pointed it at my chest. "Let's go. Both of you. I think I have it all figured out."

The clock in the hall began to chime. "And not a moment too soon," he muttered. "To the cemetery and do as I say."

He pushed us past John and out onto the porch. I stumbled and fell against Campbell. Caught by surprise, we both almost fell down the steps. I thought I heard something hit the ground at the edge of the porch but forgot about it as his fingers tightened roughly around my arm.

"Fool!" he growled in my ear. "Watch what you're doing!"

It was a dreary group that walked up to the cemetery. Daylight was fast fading. I kept my eyes on the sunset. It was the prettiest one I'd ever seen, or so it seemed to me. Maybe I was able to appreciate it more because I wasn't sure if it was the last one I'd ever see.

At the gate, I stopped. "This is it. My parent's grave is over there." I pointed to the huge stone.

"Don't stop now, sweetheart. We're just beginning," he said gleefully.

Campbell opened the gate with a flourish and bowed for us to enter. We stood in a small circle around the marker. With my eyes on the grave, where Papa rested, I murmured, "If I believed in ghosts, Campbell, I'd know Papa was here watching over us. He'd strike you dead where you stand!"

Campbell pressed the tip of his knife up against the bodice of my dress. With a flick of his wrist, he slashed the front and I watched a few drops of blood appear from the torn fabric. When I made a move to cover my wound, he brushed my hands aside.

"You're a very desirable woman, Althea. But your tongue is too acid for me. I've warned you all evening to keep quiet. Now shut up! It'll take more than a ghost to help you now." His eyes flickered over me once more, but greed for the jewels overpowered his lust. Through clenched teeth, he growled, "Get down by that marble base and start digging!"

I started to giggle hysterically. Seeing the shock on Hilda's face forced my giggles into loud guffaws of laughter.

"What's so funny?" said Campbell suspiciously.

"I was just thinking. I'm certainly in a convenient spot to be murdered. Right here in the cemetery."

Campbell stepped close and slapped me across the cheek. "Stop that! Do you want to live longer or die now?"

"What difference does it make?" I sneered. "I'm going to die anyway. It might as well be now."

Campbell let go of me to grab Hilda by the arm. He pointed the knife at her throat. "You may not care about yourself, but what about your friend?"

His gesture sobered me. Slowly I turned to the stone. On my knees, I began to dig out the moist dirt with my hands. My one ray of hope lay in Grant coming home earlier than anticipated. Otherwise my future looked bleak.

While Hilda and I dug out the dirt from under the marker, Campbell stood over us, directing us from the paper he held in his hand. "Over more to the left," he called to me. "Stay up next to the stone. I'm sure this is where he buried it."

For over an hour we dug. I leaned back to wipe a dirty hand across my face. My back ached and I was discouraged. "I don't think this is the place."

"I know it is!" he growled. "You aren't digging deep enough. Move over more to the left side."

I shrugged and began to dig again. After a time, I felt the stone move. I looked at Hilda. If the marker fell, we'd both be crushed. I moved to one side and motioned for Hilda to do the same. At least this way we would have a chance to roll out of the way. We continued to scrape away the dirt by the handful. The more we took away, the more the stone moved.

Finally I could stand it no longer. "I think we should stop. If we take out any more dirt, this marker's going to fall."

"Foolish women!" muttered Campbell. "Get out of my way!" He pushed at us, saying, "Get behind there and hold on to the stone. I want to see what you were doing wrong."

We did as told but knew we would be no match for the heavy marble should it fall. Even as we touched the stone, it moved again.

"Keep that thing steady," he called up to us, his voice muffled. A second later he shouted in triumph. "I found it! I wish I had a light. It's caught and I can't pull it free."

He had just finished speaking when we heard horses coming up the driveway. I felt weak with relief. Hilda and I both let loose of the stone and turned to watch the buggy stop in front of the house.

"They're home!" I shouted in joy, seeing Grant climb down from the carriage. "Come on, Hilda let's run."

"I'll kill you if you go," said Campbell.

We didn't pay any attention to him. Grant was home. We started to go but felt rather than saw the stone start its descent. "Watch out!" I screamed, but his greed was his undoing. He wouldn't let go of the pouch, so he was crushed by the weight of the stone.

In disbelief I watched him die, his scream of horror echoing in my ears. I turned to see Grant come through the gate. "Grant" was all I could say before fainting, my head coming to rest between Papa and Mama's graves.

CHAPTER THIRTEEN

The bag. Made of dark brown leather, it felt heavy in my hand. The memories came flooding over me. The intimidation and the fear. The calculated coldness in Campbell's eyes. His last cry of terror. Then death.

Grant knelt at my side. The night was bright with torches and lanterns. "Let's go to the house" was all he said as he carried me past all the servants. I relaxed in his arms. I was safe now. Safe from Campbell.

John's body still lay in the hall, but a blanket had been spread over him. I saw him and mumbled, "Poor old John. He tried to help me but only got himself killed."

The sheriff was sent for. The body of Campbell was removed

from the cemetery. I had the jewels clutched in my hand. All that remained was an explanation to my husband. So far he'd only seen to my welfare, but all too soon the questions would begin.

Upstairs in our room, Grant laid me on the bed. My torn dress fell back to expose my wound. The blood had dried around the angry red cut. I saw Grant's jaw harden as he stared down at me. I quickly covered myself, but I knew I had to say something. Being truthful, I murmured, "I don't know what to say first, Grant."

"What went on here tonight?" he gestured toward my hand. "I assume he was after that. It was clutched in his hand."

I nodded slowly. "Yes. Have you looked inside?"

"No. I figured it was yours."

With trembling fingers I untied the string and dumped the contents into my lap. I knew what to expect, so I wasn't nearly as surprised as Grant. I heard him suck in his breath in amazement.

The light played across the gems, making them look like a small ball of fire in my lap. Green emeralds. Red rubies. Blue sapphires. Diamonds. Iridescent opals and pearls. All the colors of the rainbow blended into a sparkling flame of fire.

I let the gems slip through my fingers like grains of sand. My voice was sad as I sighed, "These brought about the death of an innocent old man and a greedy cutthroat. If you hadn't come, Hilda and I would be dead too."

I didn't look at Grant as I spoke. I kept my eyes on my lap. "Some time ago, Papa took the family heirloom jewelry to Gus Sawyer. He wanted all the gems removed from the settings. Gus has the settings at his store now. But Papa hid the stones for me. He wanted me to marry you, but he also wanted me to have some security all my own. He told me about the jewels the day he died, but he wouldn't say where he'd hidden them. He thought he was giving me a clue, but I wasn't smart enough to figure it out. We stumbled upon it by accident tonight. I should have known Papa would have put them where he knew they would be safe." I shook my head. "He was keeping watch over them for me."

"But how did Campbell know about them?" demanded Grant. *"I* sure as hell knew nothing."

"It was the last time we were at the theater. Remember when you and Helene came back to the box? Gus was there. He spoke to me of the settings and Campbell was outside the curtain, listening to us. It wasn't a surprise to see him ride up to the house the next day."

Grant paced the room. He ran his hand over his hair in bewilderment. Finally he said, "I think I understand most of what followed. You really hated Campbell, didn't you?"

"Of course. I loathed the man. I knew he was a crook. He hated you for winning his money in that poker game. Tonight he was looking for the jewels, but he wanted to hurt you too."

"That was why you went downstairs at night?"

"Yes. I had to watch him to make sure he wasn't searching while I slept."

I sensed a deep relief in him concerning my late-night prowling, but his blue eyes remained cool. "Why didn't you come to me?" he asked. "Why didn't you trust me enough to share this?"

I was a long time in answering. I knew this would come. I took time to scoop up the stones and put them back in the pouch. I spoke softly as I picked them up. "I once thought to use these to entice you away from here. I was sure you were greedy. If you took one look at these, I knew you would leave me in peace." I glanced at him and added, "Of course I had those thoughts before I had a chance to meet you. Now I know differently."

I laid the pouch on the table and got up from the bed. I was too tense to lie still. I moved restlessly around the room. "I wanted to come to you several times, but I couldn't. We've never tried talking to each other." When Grant started to object, I said quickly, "Please see this from my side. I've been beholden to you from the start. I hadn't met you, but you were providing me with the very clothes on my back. I came to Willowcrest to meet my future husband and got off on the wrong foot." I stopped, realizing what I had said. I saw Grant's mouth draw down into those old familiar lines of bitterness.

I didn't back down. I lifted my chin and stared him straight in the eye. I repeated, "We got off on the wrong foot. Since then, we've shouted, argued, taunted and sneered at each other. But we've never been honest. At least having the jewels was something I could call my own. Nothing else is. This bedroom has nothing in it that's really mine. As I said, the clothes aren't mine. I didn't have any say in what you picked out. I just wanted one thing I could say was mine." My voice was very shaky and I stopped talking.

Tears were in my eyes. I hadn't expected him to understand. That would have been too much to hope for. When Grant didn't speak, I turned away in dejection. So that was the way it was to be.

Too tired to think of modesty, I stripped to bathe my aches and bruises. I dried the cut on my breast tenderly. It was as sore and raw as it looked. I slipped into a warm nightgown, then crawled into bed. Grant watched me silently. I couldn't read his expression. I didn't even try. I was past caring.

I suppose I fell asleep. But it was a sleep filled with nightmares. I awoke to find Grant's arms around me.

"Wake up, Althea. It's only a dream," he murmured.

I stirred, almost afraid to open my eyes. My voice trembled. "I was so frightened. I saw the stone falling, but it was me trapped under it. Not Campbell."

Grant pulled me closer, cradling my head on his shoulder. Smoothing my hair, he rocked me tenderly. "Don't be afraid. It's all over. While I'm near, no one will harm you. You have to believe in me, Althea," he urged.

I was too tired and sleepy to puzzle over his odd words.

Reassured, I snuggled closer and fell asleep to the strong beat of Grant's heart.

Time heals all wounds, or so I was told many times that next week. My bruises did fade, but the damage Campbell did to my spirit was slower to mend. I knew Grant was busy erasing all evidence of what took place downstairs. I stayed in the bedroom. I hadn't been able to bring myself to see what Campbell had done. Nothing interested me. Hilda was gone from Willowcrest. Before she left, she assured me my depression would disappear, if I gave it time. I wasn't as sure as she was.

I kept to my room. I saw Grant and Sarah. The others stayed away. I wondered if Helene grieved for her friend Campbell or if she felt guilty for asking him to the house. I didn't imagine she knew the meaning of the word "guilty." She seemed incapable of any emotion except conceit and self-indulgence. If Helene saw something she wanted, it didn't matter whom she hurt. She took it. I knew she wanted Grant and I was in her way.

By staying in the bedroom, I felt safe from her. There weren't any stairs or embankments handy. But I was still vulnerable to her devious mind. Helene might decide to shoot me or try smothering me with a pillow. These thoughts did nothing to ease my fears.

I was a bundle of nerves. All morning I'd noticed a restlessness growing inside of me. It was a lovely day outdoors. A day for walking or seeking a warm spot to soak up some sun. I tried sitting by the open window. I watched the curtains rise and fall with a gentle breeze. I was letting my favorite time of the year pass by.

The long afternoon lay before me. Empty. The thought of staying in the bedroom another day was more than I could endure. Before I could change my mind, I jumped up and tied a bonnet over my head.

I knew my leaving the room would please Grant. He hadn't

pressed me. He had been kind and thoughtful all week. At night when the nightmares set me trembling, it helped to know he was only an arm's length away. Many times the words "I love you" hung on my lips, but I didn't give in to temptation. I knew I couldn't stand to be rejected or see the pity for me in his eyes.

I found that first step outside my bedroom door wasn't as hard as I'd thought. I walked slowly to the staircase and looked down. I felt rather than heard someone near me.

I whirled around, my hand at my throat. My breath came in ragged gasps. I found Helene watching me. She was dressed in as lovely a manner as ever. In a pale shade of blue, with yards of lace and ribbon, her dress was a confection of femininity. Her hair hung down her back. It was the color of the sun and was shining just as brightly.

I felt a stab of envy beneath my fear of this woman. Helene looked so lovely, while I felt dowdy beside her. For days I'd lost interest in my appearance. I had taken to wearing some of my old mourning dresses. Not out of respect for Campbell, but because their dark somber colors suited my present mood. Now facing Helene, I knew I looked like death. It wasn't any wonder Grant treated me with courtesy instead of passion. I looked more like his Aunt Celia than his wife.

"What do you want?" I whispered hoarsely. I moved away from the stairs.

"Good morning, Althea," said Helene cheerfully. "I see you've finally come out of hiding. I was beginning to think I'd seen the last of you." Her tone implied how much this would have pleased her.

I didn't bother to answer. I kept my eyes glued to her, ready to meet any challenge she might toss to me.

"If you're going downstairs, I'll be glad to walk with you." She smiled innocently. "It would be a shame if the first day out you fell again. And this time you might not be as lucky." She reached out a hand.

I jerked away, pressing my back against the railing of the balcony. "Get away from me," I hissed. "Get away or I'll call for help."

She walked by me on down the stairs. Her laughter floated back to me. "Silly woman," she called. "I only wanted to help you."

I swallowed my hysteria, looking around the hall. I was alone. Once again her snide attitude wasn't witnessed. I felt a flash of anger. It wasn't fair. No one believed me. Even Hilda hadn't been completely convinced of my fears. If my good friend didn't believe me, how could I expect Grant or Celia to?

I waited until Helene was out of sight before I ran lightly down the stairs and out into the sunshine. Without my thinking, my feet automatically took me to the cemetery. I'd always found peace here. Could I still? I felt apprehensive. I knew his body was gone. I knew the stone had been righted. It should look the same, but it was the ghost of a memory haunting me.

As I climbed the slight incline to the bluff, my breathing came quickly. I knew it wasn't from the exercise but anxiousness.

I hesitated at the gate before stepping into the enclosure. Taking deep breaths, I walked to the stone. My hand trembled as I touched the slab of marble. The warmth of the day hadn't penetrated its coolness. It felt smooth and firm under my hand.

I closed my mind to that awful night. Instead I brought forth all the good times. Papa had been right. We had found pleasure here. The warm spring days when we had picnicked here. Then later in the fall on a crisp day, we had raked away all the dead leaves, making the graves neat for winter.

I began to feel a lightness of spirit. Nothing had changed. This place still held tranquility and solitude for me. Even a man like Campbell couldn't destroy that.

I didn't know how long I'd been gone from the house, but the time had been well spent. I had come to terms with my fears. I was ready to face what was in store for me. I had Helene to deal with. This time I would be prepared. She could strike at any time. I would fight her for my life.

Looking around me, I saw the sun beginning to dip behind the horizon. Many times in the past, I'd stood at this spot and marveled at the changes sundown created. Leaves rustled as tiny animals scurried home to settle in for the night.

A week ago I hadn't known for sure I would see another dusk. Now I stood gaping at this marvelous phenomenon. As the sun disappeared, I saw the world bathed in a bright rosy pink glow.

I walked back to the house in the twilight of the evening. I loved my home, but it would never be the same if I didn't have Grant to share it with me. It was Grant who made everything right. I had let him remain ignorant of my feelings long enough. I had to tell him how I felt. I would be taking a chance on rejection, but tonight I would do it. I'd be honest. After all, those had been my words to him.

My heart felt light as I stepped into the hallway. Good smells were coming from the dining room. If I hurried, I would be able to eat with my husband. I tossed my bonnet on the newel post and smoothed my hair as I walked to the open dining room door.

Grant, Celia and Helene sat at the table. Grant's broad back was to me. He was talking. "Father seems in good spirits today. We had a good long talk, though it was one-sided. I believe he and I are closer." He laughed shortly. "Perhaps it's because this is the first time I've had the opportunity to tell him everything I've always wanted to."

Celia nodded her head. "I've noticed a change in Arthur. He seems more at ease. Quieter. He hasn't gotten agitated for many days. He seems to be content to rest and let us come visit him. He adores Althea. I have every hope he'll live a long and happy life."

From where I was standing, I had a clear view of Helene. At

Celia's words, I saw a look of fright cross her features. So fleeting was the look that I was left asking myself if I'd imagined it.

"Darling," Helene said to Grant, "where's that tardy wife of yours? I thought she would join us for dinner." Helene sighed in bewilderment. "I really don't understand Althea, Grant. This isolation of hers is odd. You say she hated Thomas, and yet she dresses in black and refuses to see us. It's almost like she's in mourning." She dabbed at her dry eyes. "He was my friend. If anyone should be upset, it's me."

"You *thought* he was a friend," Grant corrected her. "He took advantage of your innocent nature. As for Althea, we have to treat her kindly. We don't know half the things Campbell said to her and Hilda. He was a ruthless man. He threatened them both with death and even took a shot at Hilda. It was a frightening time for Althea, but she's strong. I have every confidence she'll bring herself out of this depression she's in. Until then we all have to be understanding and sympathetic."

I thanked Grant silently. I'd heard enough. I put a smile on my face and walked into the dining room. It warmed my heart to see the pleasure spread across Grant's face. Aunt Celia was obviously delighted with my entrance, but Helene didn't bother to hide her dislike. I bent to kiss Aunt Celia's cheek. Nodding to Helene, I touched Grant lightly on the shoulder.

"I feel better today. I decided to join you for dinner."

Helene looked at my wrinkled black dress and smudged face. She sniffed. "The least you could have done was to wash your face and put on a more cheerful dress. You look like one of the servants, Althea. Only they're cleaner."

I blushed with embarrassment. "I'm sorry," I murmured to Grant. "I've been outside. I didn't want to take the time to change. I was afraid of missing dinner with you." I started to my feet. "I'll have a tray sent to me upstairs."

Grant glared at Helene while pressing me back to my chair.

"My dear. We want you here. As for your face . . ." He reached over to rub at my chin softly. "There," he said, satisfied. "You look just fine. Let's finish our meal," he added firmly to everyone.

I bent over my plate to hide my smile of pleasure. Grant was the perfect husband that evening at the table. He saw to my every desire. He included me in the conversation. His attention was like a fine wine. It went to my head, making me dizzy with excitement and joy. I was looking forward to talking to him later.

When we finished our meal and retired to the study, I was leery of entering this room. It was Grant's warm hand at my back that gave me the courage to face what was ahead.

I looked around and breathed a sigh of relief. The old desk still stood where it always had. An exact replica was being built and would be delivered in another week or so. A new chair sat behind the desk. It was so much like the old one that I was able to persuade myself it was the same. Books were back on the shelves. The section Campbell had pulled down was hanging where it belonged. I sat down, content to sip the tea Sarah placed before me.

The conversation flowed around me. I listened politely. Aunt Celia had gone up to bed after dinner. I was ready to follow suit but hesitated leaving Helene and Grant alone. They were laughing easily together about Whitmore Halls and its friends and neighbors.

Since I'd never seen the Halls or met the people, I just smiled pleasantly, completely left out of this conversation. I knew this was exactly Helene's plan. It was she who had started the conversation as soon as we were seated.

I was ready to admit defeat and go up when Grant turned to me.

He sighed, "I guess we had better say good night. I see Althea can hardly keep her eyes open."

"I *am* tired," I admitted. Then, wanting to be kind, I added as a token gesture, "Don't feel you have to come up too, Grant. Finish your drink. I'll go on ahead." I almost choked as he poured himself another brandy.

"All right," he said. "If you don't mind. I'll be up shortly."

There was nothing for me to do but leave the room. As I passed Helene, I saw the smug look on her face. I smiled pleasantly, looking unconcerned on the outside, but I was furious with her and myself on the inside.

In the bedroom I found my bath ready. I removed my clothes and was soon luxuriating in the tub's warm depths. It helped soothe away my irritation. After I'd toweled off, I settled in bed, ready to wait for Grant.

An hour passed, then two. Sick at heart, I finally admitted he wasn't coming up to bed. I blew out the lamp. In the darkness I tried to ignore the kaleidoscope of pictures my jealous imagination conjured up.

What was keeping him? My eyes grew heavy. As I dropped off to sleep, I was thankful I hadn't given in to my impetuous feelings. I'd let his kind and friendly manner rule my good judgment. I should have known it was just part of his role of dutiful husband.

I sighed remorsefully, "That had been our plan." I'd almost lost my pride, but it wouldn't happen again. I had everything figured out now. I would guard against any more disappointment and pain. No one could hurt me again if I was prepared, and I would be prepared from now on.

CHAPTER FOURTEEN

After the night Grant failed to come to bed, I threw myself into work around the house and garden. I pushed him out of my mind, or so I tried to convince myself. Throughout the day I was fine. I cleaned and brought Willowcrest back to its former loveliness. With everything in place, memories of Campbell were beginning to blur with time. I'd even stopped having nightmares. An excuse for Grant to touch me was gone too.

It was these long lonely nights that affected me. Grant was only a few inches away, yet he might have been in another part of the house. I treated him politely. I saw the question in his eyes at my odd behavior, but he didn't ask me anything. I was glad. I didn't have an answer for him. How could I explain the hurt I was feeling? If I did, he would know how vulnerable I was.

Grant had his own worries. Whitmore Halls had been left unattended too long. He felt unable to go himself, so he sent Raymond. Arthur was regaining his strength. He was able to sit by the window for long periods of time, but his speech was still incomprehensible. Unable to go home and resume his position as master, Arthur was content to leave the details up to his son.

With Arthur out of danger, I put forth a plan I'd been contemplating since returning to Willowcrest. I wanted to give a party. For once Helene and I were in complete agreement. Grant wasn't very enthusiastic with my idea, but he didn't forbid me. He was very generous in giving me control of everything, from the decorations to the food for the buffet.

Separately we each made up a list of guests. All together there would be a total of forty people invited. This looked to be a monumental feat for me, but I felt up to it. I had Agnes' help with the food and Sarah's help with the cleaning and decorating. Everything was going well. Even Helene offered some suggestions that I couldn't turn down.

I tried to stay away from her, but she was everywhere, overseeing my arrangements. I tried to ignore her, but it was difficult to ignore her exhibitions with Grant. Yesterday I'd gone to the stable to ask Grant about music for dancing. I walked into the tack room, looking at the paper in my hand. When I glanced up, I found Helene gazing up into Grant's face, adoration written on hers. I didn't wait to hear any excuses. I choked out some remark and ran back to the house.

Behind me I heard Grant calling to me, but I didn't stop. I fought the tears away. I wouldn't let him see how much his infidelity hurt. From that time on, I was very careful to avoid other chance meetings. My surprise visit to the stable only seemed to please Helene. She was getting more and more daring in front of me. But to everyone else she was the model houseguest.

I had another worry. It was so frightening that if I sat down and really let myself think about it, I would go to pieces. Campbell's gun was missing. The knife had been found near his body but not the gun. The sheriff had questioned all of us. I'd thought and thought, trying to remember when I'd last seen it. He had held a knife to my throat. It had been the blade of the knife that had cut my dress and wounded my breast. Had he dropped it? In the excitement would it have gone unnoticed? Who had found it?

It was this last question that made my heart flutter. The thought of a gun in Helene's hand was appalling. I had seen the hatred in her eyes. I knew she wouldn't hesitate to use it.

Perhaps it was this thought that kept me close to the house and away from anyplace where she could hide and fire at me. Worry about my fate made me unusually alert to things going on around me. It sharpened my wits, making me aware of a change in Grant.

At first I didn't know what to make of him. A warm smile. A gentle touch. Even when we were alone, I found him to be considerate. This attention made me uneasy. I felt I was being manipulated. But for what reason? Was he up to something? Was he being kind to me before letting the ax fall? Had Helene won at last?

My only course of action seemed to be to avoid him. I knew this might be accomplished during the day, but what about the night? For the entire morning, I had stayed out of Grant's way. I tried to keep Sarah with me at all times. When Grant came around, I nodded but continued to give Sarah orders. Once I thought it was all over when Grant came stomping into the room. Curtly he dismissed Sarah.

"I'd like a word with you, Althea," he said.

"I'm really very busy, Grant," I murmured. "Perhaps later . . ."

"No! I think this is an excellent time to get this out in the open," he began, but Helene came into the room.

"Darling, Auntie's calling for you. She says the latch on one of the windows is stuck. Would you see to it?"

"Get someone else," snapped Grant, hardly looking at her.

"Who?" she persisted. "With John gone . . ." She let her voice trail off. We all knew what she meant. I hadn't had the heart to permanently replace John, but I knew I would have to do it soon.

"All right," growled Grant. He went to the door but turned back to me. I couldn't meet his eyes.

"I'll see you later," he said in an ominous tone.

I nodded my head, but I knew he wouldn't. Not if I could

help it. He sounded much too serious. I didn't like what he had said, "Get this out in the open."

I hurried to the kitchen. Here I felt safe. I'd never known Grant to come here. I perched myself on a stool and took out my memo pad. For the next hour, Agnes and I went over the list of foods for the party. With forty guests the amount would be staggering, but the assortment had to be of a variety to suit everyone's palate.

"I think we need to add a few more pastries, Agnes. Everyone has a sweet tooth. Perhaps some of those tiny cakes that you ice in pastel colors?"

"That would be nice, miss. They're tasty and look pretty on the silver platters," agreed Agnes.

I brushed back a stray curl that tickled my cheek. "Are you sure we have gotten in enough supplies? I think we need to check everything once more."

"Very well, Miss Althea. But I think we're about ready. All we have to do is get everything cooked and baked."

I had to laugh as I thought of all the cakes, pies, breads, meats and other dishes. "Only, Agnes?" I questioned humorously.

"You're working too hard, Althea," said a deep voice from the door.

I jumped at the unexpected sight of Grant lounging against the doorway. His eyes held a teasing light as they moved slowly over my blushing face.

"I don't want you so tired you can't enjoy your own party."

"I'm fine," I declared stiffly. "Did you want to see me?"

"Yes. I want to talk to you." He glanced at Agnes and raised his eyebrow. "Let's go to the study." He turned to lead the way but stopped. "No. Helene's in there." His face was thoughtful. "I know. Why don't we go to the—"

The back door opened and a workman shouted, "There you are Mr. Whitmore. That new heifer you bought is getting ready to drop her first calf. I think she's in trouble!"

Grant looked from the workman to me. He was undecided. He finally sighed heavily. "All right. I'm coming." To me he repeated firmly, "I have to talk to you!"

"I'll be around here somewhere," I called to his departing back. I was getting curious. He had been trying to talk to me all morning. I knew he would soon get his chance. I couldn't stay out of his way much longer. I was tempted to hide from him but knew that was childish. I couldn't hide for the rest of my life.

This time he was gone so long that I'd almost forgotten about his threat of a talk. Grant came to the kitchen again, to the pantry. I'd gone inside to check on supplies with Agnes. He stood in the door, blocking my light. I turned to him and asked, "Well? How is the cow?"

"Fine, fine," he said impatiently. "She's the proud mother of a large bull calf."

"Good," I said. We faced each other, very ill at ease. I said, "It's dark in here. Let's go back into the kitchen."

I tried to brush past Grant, but he took my arm. I stopped to look up at him. He opened his mouth to speak, but Sarah came rushing up to me.

"Miss Althea, come look at the linens. I've laid them out on the dining room table. See if you think they'll do."

"Excuse me," I murmured to Grant, who was tugging all the while on my arm.

"No!" he exploded.

I cringed away from his fury. Sarah and Agnes moved out of his way as he stormed into the kitchen. He ranted like a madman.

"I've been trying to have a word with you all day," he shouted. "All I've heard is this confounded party. I'm tired of it!" He suddenly became aware of the amazement on our faces. He stopped his angry pacing and smiled ruefully. "I'd like to speak to my wife." He glared around the room. "Would you ladies excuse us? If anyone comes looking for us, don't tell them where we are. That's an order!"

"And where will we be?" I asked as he took my arm and escorted me briskly out the door.

"I don't know," grinned Grant. "We could be anywhere."

I smiled timidly at him. He seemed in high spirits. Again I felt a moment of anxiety but pushed it aside. He was about to tell me something and there wasn't any way I could stop him. He held my arm in a tight grip.

Grant led me along the path by the river. Under cover of the willows, he tucked my hand under his arm and we strolled along silently. Covertly I stole glances at his handsome profile. He was so thoughtful. I wondered what was on his mind. As we walked I noticed a chill in the air. In the distance thunder rumbled.

"I think it's going to rain," I said.

Grant glanced up at the gathering storm clouds. "It'll take a while to reach us," he predicted, but he was wrong. He had barely spoken when the first drops began to fall.

I sheltered my head with my folded hands. "We'll have to hurry back to the house or we're going to get soaked."

"No!" shouted Grant. He stood on the bank of the mighty river and shook his clenched fist at the sky. "Everything and everyone is plotting against me! First Helene, then that cow and now the weather. It's enough to make a man crazy." Pulling me by the hand, he started to run away from the house.

I pushed my wet hair out of my eyes and yelled, "Where are we going?"

"I don't know, but I'm not going back to the house. It's like a circus there. A man can't have any privacy."

I dug in my heels, forcing Grant to come to a halt. I looked in his eyes, searching his face. "Why do you want privacy?" I demanded. I expected him to say anything, but I'd never expected to see my strong and handsome husband blush.

"Grant?" I asked softly. "Why do you want to talk to me?"

He stared over my shoulder. "I thought we would have that honest talk you mentioned the other night."

I raised a hand to touch his jaw lightly. He turned his head so his lips rubbed across my fingers. "An honest talk?" I asked gently.

His blue eyes bored into mine. I was breathless. I knew I was seeing something very special in his eyes. I couldn't be wrong. This time it was I who took his hand and began to run.

"Where are we going?" he called into the wind.

"A place where we won't be disturbed" was all I could say.

There was a storm raging inside of me as well as around me. I felt sure I knew what Grant wanted to say, and I knew just the place for it. It wasn't far and no one knew of its existence but me. Papa had ordered me never to go alone. I wasn't alone. I had a very special man with me. I turned to smile brightly at him. My heart turned over as he returned my smile.

The path wound down toward the river, stopping at a pile of rocks and brush. I moved away the dried brush, revealing a large hole. Over the roar of the rain and the swiftly moving river below us, I called, "This is my cave."

"Is it safe?" asked Grant.

"Of course. Come in."

I went in first, wondering what time had done to the inside. The tunnel was narrow, but I could hear Grant scrambling along behind me. It was always a surprise to find myself suddenly in a large underground chamber made of stone, it was as silent as a tomb.

I jumped up from my knees and clapped the dirt from my hand. Gesturing around the room, I curtsied, "You wanted privacy. Here you are."

Grant looked around him in astonishment. "I had no idea this existed."

"I know. I found it years ago as a child. Papa forced me to

promise never to come here alone. He was afraid I might slip and fall into the river, but I was always careful."

Grant had gone to a small table sitting in the middle of the room. "What was this for?" he asked.

"Papa was very indulgent," I admitted with a laugh. "He let me bring some articles down from the house. I brought some chairs too. Later he helped me bring down an old trunk." My eyes sparkled with excitement. "Wait. I wonder if my treasure is still inside."

Grant hunched his shoulders. "It's cold in here."

"I know, and it's damp too but it's out of the rain." I stopped talking as I opened the lid of the trunk. I pulled out a jar with some matches in it. A stub of a candle was still usable. There was a feather pillow and two quilts. I handed one to Grant and said, "They smell musty, but at least they're dryer than we are and warmer."

Grant took my offered quilt and grinned almost leeringly. "I know a better way to keep warm."

A day or even an hour ago, I might have turned away from the invitation in his eye, but not this time. I'd waited too long to become prim and proper now. I smiled my acceptance of his proposal.

He gathered me in his arms. I turned my head to meet his kiss. Gone were my inhibitions. I loved my husband and though he hadn't spoken the words, I knew he cared for me too. I pressed closer, wanting him, feeling his need for me. As our kiss ended, Grant spoke breathlessly, "That helped get the blood circulating again."

I laughed softly, enjoying his strong arms around me. I leaned back and said, "Do you want to sit down?"

Grant snorted, "Sit? Hardly!"

In the semidarkness I knew his eyes were twinkling dangerously. He kissed my lips again. He stepped away from me and I felt his playfulness vanish. Grant stood before me, his proud head bowed. My heart went out to him, but I remained silent.

Lightly he traced a finger along the length of my jaw. He cupped my chin in his strong hand, raising my face to his.

"You wanted us to speak honestly, Althea. I can't be more honest when I say, I love you. I want and need you to share my life."

Tears gathered in my eyes, which he quickly kissed away. "Are you upset?" he asked in concern.

With trembling fingers I touched his face. "You've made me very happy. I'd given up hope of you ever caring for me."

I had ached so long for this moment. I had his words of love. We were married. Nothing else mattered. We were two people alone in the world. Our world. As our bodies pressed tightly together, I finally knew what being loved meant. I'd found a fulfillment I'd always known existed but had never tasted. I was loved.

In the afterglow of our lovemaking, I lay in the circle of his arm. We spoke softly, afraid to break the spell surrounding us.

"When did you first realize you cared for me?" I asked.

I felt him lift his shoulder in a shrug. "I don't know. It was before Campbell came. I knew I cared deeply for you, or it wouldn't have hurt so bad when I thought you were in love with him."

"I've never felt this way about any man," I murmured. "I didn't even know feelings like this existed."

Grant chuckled softly. "I'm sorry I waited so long to tell you how I feel."

"Why did you wait?"

"I was afraid to admit it to myself, let alone to you." He shifted his position so he could look down at me. "Do you remember that night when we had been to the theater. I carried you upstairs and put you on the bed?"

I remembered only too well. I nodded my head.

"When I looked down at you lying there, I was overwhelmed with desire for you. My feelings took me by surprise. I was scared of them. I hadn't planned to fall in love with you. I went downstairs and tried to drown my new love in a whiskey bottle. The next day Campbell came. I didn't know what to think. Then he died and you were depressed. I didn't want to tell you then. When you finally showed signs of returning to your old self, you changed toward me. You became cool and detached. I decided you didn't care about me. It took me all week to work up enough courage to approach you. I was afraid you would reject me, but I'd survived that before. I knew I had to find out how our marriage stood."

I sighed, "We've worked at cross-purposes, haven't we? I've loved you for so long. My loving glances and words of love weren't all an act for your family. I loved you even before they came. It almost broke my heart when you kissed me in your study that day in front of Raymond and I realized it was only an act."

"My poor darling," Grant said, pulling me tightly to him. "I had no idea you felt that way."

His lips searched for mine. When I was released, any hurt I'd felt was forgotten. All except one question. I asked, "Where were you the entire night about a week ago? When I left you in the study you were finishing your glass of brandy. I waited up for you, wanting to speak to you, but you never came."

Grant was silent as he thought. "It was that next morning I noticed a coolness about you. You thought I was with Helene, didn't you?" he demanded.

"Yes," I admitted, not meeting his eyes. "What else was I to think?"

"Why not the truth? I was needed out in the barn."

I sat up, filled with relief. "Is that where you were?"

"I sent Helene up to tell you that I would be very late coming to bed. That new shipment of heifers arrived that night. They are worth too much money to turn loose in the pasture. I wanted to make sure they were fed and bedded properly."

"You sent Helene up to tell me?" I repeated.

"Yes," he said. "I suppose she didn't tell you?"

"No. I saw no one."

"It wasn't only we who were at cross-purposes," said Grant with a frown. "We had some help. I'll have to have a talk with her."

I wanted to tell him several more things that had happened, but I didn't want to bring Helene into our hideaway. My cave was filled with lovely memories. To introduce the subject of Helene was to ruin our newfound enjoyment of each other.

The time slipped swiftly by. We were content to stay in each others arms, talking softly of our love, our hopes and dreams. It was with reluctance that we decided it was time to go back to the house. I was sure we had been missed. Maybe we were even being searched for.

We quickly rolled up the blankets and got dressed. Grant went on out the tunnel first. I lingered for a minute. How could such a cold, damp and dark hole in the side of the bluff hold such warmth and happiness? I knew that it wasn't where we were that mattered. It was the man I was with. Grant could make even a cave seem like heaven. With a smile of sheer happiness, I crawled out to join my husband.

The house looked warm and inviting as it came into view. We began to run the last few yards, bursting in the front doors, laughing. We quickly sobered when faced with the group waiting in the hall. Helene and Aunt Celia were grim-faced, as were the servants around them. A stable hand stepped forward to speak.

"Looks like you folks got worried for nothing. They aren't hurt, just cold and wet." He suddenly chuckled, "They sure seem pleased over something." Still grinning, he went quickly out the door and out into the chilly night air.

Grant frowned after the man. His frown deepened as he turned back to the silent group. "Don't look so disapproving. We're fine. We got caught in the rain and had to take shelter."

Helene stepped forward and said, "But the rain ended an hour ago. Where have you been?"

Grant hugged me tightly to his side. "We were talking and didn't realize it had stopped raining." To forestall any more questions, he added, "Agnes, send up a tray of tea for my wife and a brandy for me. We'll both want a hot bath too. As you all can see, we are very wet and muddy."

Once we got away from all the looks, I dissolved into gales of laughter. "Did you see their faces? We really have them puzzled. They don't know what to make of us."

Grant grinned and pulled me near. "Did I tell you I love you?"

"Mmm," I murmured, nuzzling his ear. "I think so, but say it again. I don't think I could ever get tired of those three little words."

"I love you, Althea," he whispered softly. Then he began to show me just how much he did care. I was left without a doubt as to my husband's feelings.

CHAPTER FIFTEEN

My days were filled with thoughts of the approaching party. My nights were filled with Grant. I watched my love smooth away the deep lines of bitterness that had become a part of his expression. I watched him smile more and laugh easily. I loved him before, but as he changed and mellowed, I found myself falling in love all over again. He was a fierce protector. A teacher too. He showed me how to please him as he worked his enchantment on me. His love brought a glow to my cheeks and put a sparkle to my eyes. I was nervous about the party, but he kept my feet firmly on the ground. His praise and firm confidence in me made me feel I could take on the world. He made me strong, except where Helene was concerned.

She was the one dark cloud on my otherwise bright horizon. I'd tried to talk to Grant about Helene, but he calmly dismissed her as unimportant. He readily agreed that Helene felt an infatuation for him, but he was sure she would get over it now that he was so obviously in love with me.

I listened to him and felt reassured when with him, but when I was alone I remembered all her threats. Then there was the missing gun. I could remember it so well, cradled in Campbell's hand. It was the sort of weapon Helene would covet. It was rich-looking and shiny, but most of all it was deadly.

I tried to push all my fears away, but Helene didn't help. There was a strangeness about her these days. It began the evening of the storm, when Grant and I had spoken of our love. Helene sensed a drastic change in our relationship. I expected rage and even more calculated scenes, but her manner was almost passive. Grant was the first to point out he'd been right. Helene had given up.

Several days had passed since she had singled him out for her unwanted attention. But I wasn't as sure as he. I couldn't have judged her so wrongly. She was marking time, taking walks and reading quietly. She was waiting.

If I was uncomfortable with this new Helene, Aunt Celia was greatly agitated. The two of them spoke often together. Aunt Celia always seemed to be pleading with Helene. I tried to hear what was said between them, but at my approach they would change the subject.

As Grant and I dressed for dinner, the evening before the party, I was unusually quiet.

Grant came up behind me. He put his arms around me. "Are you worried about the party?" he murmured in my ear.

I laughed self-consciously. "It's always at the back of my mind, but right now I'm thinking about Helene's odd behavior."

Grant moved away to shake his head. "Why? She's just facing the fact that I adore my wife."

"I don't know," I said, unconvinced.

Grant stared at me. "I've been thinking about what you've said. The only way to convince you is to show you you're wrong."

"How can you do that?" I asked.

"I have a plan. When we go downstairs, you go along with whatever I say," he said mysteriously.

"What are you going to do?" I was worried. I didn't like that gleam in his eyes.

"You agree with me and I'll show you how wrong you are."

I tried to question him, but he would say no more. I was uneasy. I didn't know what Grant planned. As we entered the study, we found Helene and Celia already there. They were arguing softly. Before they noticed us, I heard Helene say, "You'll stand beside me. You always have."

Then she saw us. She quickly spoke, cutting off Celia's reply. "Good evening. You'll have to excuse us. We didn't wait for you but have already poured us a glass of wine."

I pondered Helene's odd remark as Grant handed me a glass of wine. He was in a jovial mood, teasing Aunt Celia and reminiscing about the time when he was a little boy. I watched him, wondering what this was all leading to. I knew as soon as Celia gave him an opening.

"You were a terror," she laughed. "Such mischief you got into. I wonder what your own children will be like."

Grant smiled broadly. He crossed the room to my side, where he smiled proudly. "We won't have long to wait, **Auntie**. Althea and I think we're soon to be blessed with a child."

My sharp intake of breath was lost under Aunt Celia's whoop of joy. "My dear," she cried, "what wonderful news. I'd so hoped we would be hearing this from you." She smothered Grant in a tight embrace. For a moment I was left to stare into Helene's eyes. Gone was her indifference of past days. Her eyes smoldered with hostility.

I shrank back, afraid. Helene turned to pour herself another glass of wine. I was amazed at the calmness of her voice.

"Let's drink a toast to the mother to be," she said serenely.

Grant's hand pressed down on my shoulder. I knew he wanted me to notice her complete and absolute unconcern. I tried to smile up at him. His announcement took my breath away. That coupled with the loathing I'd seen in Helene's eyes made my composure very fragile. I shivered as if chilled.

Celia noticed and asked anxiously, "Are you all right, child?"

"Yes," I smiled. "I'm just tired."

"You take care of yourself, Althea," remarked Helene over her glass. "You won't want to disappoint Grant and lose this baby."

I searched her face for the malice I knew was hidden by her kind words, but I could find none. This was even more terrifying than open hostility. I was faced with a woman able to show deep concern for me while all the time wishing me dead. Had she ranted and raved after Grant's foolish announcement, I'd have proof she hadn't changed. She was too smart for that.

I caught sight of my reflection and saw my white dress was a match for my pasty complexion. I reached up to pinch my cheeks but tipped my wineglass. The red liquor spilled down the bodice of my dress, soaking it. I jumped up quickly. In the mirror it looked like blood. I stood there seeing the stain and hearing the sympathetic voices around me, but it was as if Helene and I were the only ones in the room. Our eyes locked. For a second I couldn't look away from her knowing gaze. She slowly nodded her head as if satisfied with what she saw.

I mumbled an excuse and stumbled from the room. In the bedroom I threw myself on the bed. I couldn't cry. Grant had wanted to set my mind at ease, but he had sealed my fate. I knew Helene was planning to kill me. This time it wasn't to be a spur-of-the-moment thing. She had planned the time and the place. Now she was biding her time. She was in control. I didn't know how to stop her.

The day of the party dawned bright and clear. Hilda arrived to spend the weekend and to help with last-minute details. I stayed with her or the servants all day. I looked for shadows behind every closed door. I was tense and jumpy. Everyone assumed it was nerves before the big ordeal. I didn't tell them differently. Who would believe me?

Helene stayed in the background all day. I felt her eyes on me at odd times. When I turned around, I'd find her smiling that slow benevolent smile. I'd turn away quickly, but seeing her confidence would do its damage. I shivered with fear. We were like a cat and a mouse. All day she was pushing me. Now she was gently nudging me into a corner. Soon she would pounce. When that happened I would be so demoralized I couldn't fight back.

I tried to put her out of my mind. For a time I was successful. Helene helped by leaving the house. Relaxed, I walked around Willowcrest, trying to see everything through my guest's eyes. It all sparkled from a thorough cleaning. Bouquets of flowers were all over the house. Their fragrance perfumed the air. Agnes was adding her own good smells to the festive occasion.

The dining room was lovely. We had searched the attics for large bowls and platters we didn't normally use. They were black from disuse, but we polished them until they gleamed. Set on the white linen tablecloths, the silver acted as many mirrors, reflecting the bright colors of the flowers. The ballroom was ready to receive its dancers and the musicians had arrived and were tuning up on a raised platform Grant had constructed for the occasion. Everything was ready. I was free to dress.

I was anxious to try on my new gown. I'd had one specially made for the party and was proud of the way I looked. I'd left the dress hanging on my armoire. I hurried into the room only to come to a stop just inside the door. What was left of my lovely dress hung where I'd left it. Someone had savagely ripped it to shreds. I screamed my outrage and shock. I heard feet pounding up the stairs. I met Grant at the door.

"Look," I said, "look at my lovely dress."

"My God," he said, "who would do such a terrible thing?"

Before I could say a word, Helene came into the room. I turned on her fiercely, ready to denounce her as the culprit. I saw her eyes widen in surprise. I closed my mouth. What was this? Another one of her fine performances? Yet I could almost feel her amazement.

"What happened?" she asked.

Grant whirled around, his face granite hard. "What do you know of this destruction?"

"Nothing," she said, shaking her head. "This is terrible."

I heard the ring of truth in her words. I looked back at the dress. If Helene hadn't done it, who had? Hilda came to put her arm around me.

"It's only a dress, Althea," she said in way of comfort.

I could only gulp loudly. My throat was too full of tears to speak.

Grant urged everyone out so we could be alone. His face was full of concern. "Do you want to call this evening off?"

"No," I said, striving for a light tone. "I can't throw away all our hard work and this food just for a single dress." My voice trembled, but I held my head high. "We have guests coming in another hour. I have to find a dress to wear."

He put his arm around me. I wanted to cling to him, but I willed myself to be strong. I knew before this night was over something terrible would happen. My dress was just the beginning. I prayed everyone I loved would be safe.

I moved reluctantly out of Grant's arms. "I think I'll wear the gold dress I wore on our wedding night and I'll wear the topaz necklace," I added.

Grant seemed pleased with my choice, as was Gus Sawyer, when he and the others began to arrive. Gus' eyes glowed with pleasure as he saw his artwork around my neck.

Gus' eyes twinkled humorously as he teased, "Such a lovely necklace, my dear. Was it made by anyone I know?"

Those near us laughed good-naturedly at his words. This seemed to set the mood for the beginning of the evening. I felt safe among my forty guests. Even Helene with her devious nature couldn't kill me with this many witnesses around. I began to enjoy myself. Everything was going very well. The compliments were numerous and sincere. The guests filled my home with laughter and loud conversation. I saw to their comforts and was introduced to many of Grant's friends and business acquaintances.

For a while I kept an eye on Helene. She was constantly surrounded by admirers. She danced and flirted outrageously with all the men. Young or old, married or single, it didn't seem to matter. Because she was occupied, I was free. I forgot about her and danced with my husband.

"Well?" I asked. "Do you think it's a success?"

His eyes rested on my lips, giving me the feeling I'd just been kissed. "I think *you're* a success, my darling. Everything is perfect. I don't think there's a man here who doesn't envy what I have."

I blushed with pleasure but demurred, "I'm sure it's Willowcrest. It has that effect on people. They would do anything to win it." I gazed up at him through my lashes.

Grant leaned back to stare at me. "Is that what you think?"

"Isn't that why you married me?" My tone was teasing, but I waited anxiously for his answer.

He took me seriously. "You may not like what I'm going to say, but it is the truth. I married you for several reasons. Among them was this house. You have to understand that no man can make me do something I'm not of a mind to. I had seen you several times. You suited my purpose." He gave my waist a tight squeeze and a warm smile to soften his words. "My darling, you were plain and old enough to have forgotten a younger woman's foolish fancies. That was what I wanted. I wanted a wife. A man needs a wife to keep other predatory females away. He also needs a hostess for any parties he might give. You were used to this house and to the neighbors. I thought you would be an asset to me. I wanted a wife to bow down to my lordly ways, to be a servant to my demands. Someone to see but never to be heard. I didn't think I needed a woman around here, as such. Especially not a woman I'd fall deeply in love with."

"I must have been a disappointment to you," I said.

Grant raised his eyebrows. "A disappointment? My darling, you overwhelmed me. You took it upon yourself to come out here uninvited. Once here, you did nothing obediently. You looked down your little nose at me. You did as you wanted and didn't look to me for a thing." He laughed and hugged me closely. "A disappointment? At first perhaps but my own true love now. I wish your father knew what a fine matchmaker he was."

"It would please him," I said.

We danced around the room again, then I excused myself. It would soon be time for the dining room doors to open. I wanted to make sure my hair was in place.

On the stairs, I looked back to see Helene in the center of a group of male admirers. If she noticed me leaving the room, she didn't show any sign. I hurried upstairs. It took a short time to check my hair and powder my nose. I was ready to go back down when a knock sounded on the door.

I felt a moment of fear but pushed it aside. I opened the door and found a young girl. "Yes," I said kindly. She was obviously in awe of me.

"Ma'am, one of the maids wants to see you out by the icehouse. She says you're running out of ice."

"Ice?" I repeated. "Why didn't she come?"

"I don't know," she mumbled.

I looked at her, recognizing her as one of the maids we had hired for the evening. "Who was it?" I asked.

"She said her name was Sarah, ma'am. She says she works here all the time."

"Oh, Sarah," I said in relief. "Tell her I'll be there shortly." The girl scurried away. I stood looking after her, shaking my head. Celia stepped from across the hall. With a wry smile, I said, "That poor girl acts terrified of me."

"What did she want?" Celia asked. "I heard her mention something about ice."

I quickly explained, my eyes straying to the hall, where my guests could be seen circulating.

"Let me take care of it for you, my dear. You're anxious to get back downstairs."

"Oh no. I couldn't let you do that."

"Please," she said. "You aren't really out of ice, are you?"

"I don't see how. The house should be nearly full. Summer isn't even here. I'm sure it's just a misunderstanding. I'll go set it straight."

Celia put a cold hand on my arm. "I want to do this for you, Althea. You're needed downstairs with your guests. Let me see to it."

I wavered. Celia spoke urgently. "I'd like to do it. You've been kind to me. It shouldn't take any time. As you say, it's just a silly misunderstanding."

I was puzzled by her insistence to do this but forgot about her and the problem when I saw an old friend of mine. I smiled and waved to her, at the same time saying to Celia, "All right, Auntie. It's kind of you. But if you have any trouble, let me know. It's too hot tonight to let my guests go without ice for their drinks."

"Don't worry, child. I'll take care of everything. You go enjoy yourself."

I'd already dismissed it from my mind as I crossed the hall

and took Martha's arm. It had been months since I'd seen her. I wanted to introduce her to my husband. We found him with a plate heaped high with food. Martha brought her husband and we all settled down for a good long chat.

I'd forgotten about the ice and any trouble there might be until much later. I happened to be passing through the hall when I caught sight of Aunt Celia going slowly up the stairs. I excused myself and hurried after her. I caught up with her outside her bedroom.

"Aunt Celia," I called. She didn't seem to hear me, so I touched her on the arm. She turned slowly, as if in a daze. I was shocked at the pallor of her skin. "What is it?" I asked. "Has something happened?"

She shook her head. "No, my dear. I took care of everything. You don't have anything to fear ever again."

"Fear?" I repeated blankly. "You mean the ice?"

"Ice?" She looked mixed up. Then her face cleared. "Oh yes. The ice. Just a misunderstanding, like we thought. You don't have to worry."

I felt her shivering under my hand. She swayed on her feet. "Are you all right?" I asked again. "You look upset. Did someone say something to you?"

"I'm fine, my dear," she said, patting my hand. "I'm tired. You won't think badly of me if I go to bed early." She smiled sadly. "I don't think anyone will miss an old lady."

I hugged her briefly and whispered, "I'll miss you, but you go ahead. I don't want you to get sick."

She nodded her head and almost stumbled into her room. I stood undecided. Did she need a doctor? She hadn't complained of any pain. Perhaps all she needed was a good night's rest. I shrugged and went back to join the bright lights and noise.

It was some time later when I noticed Helene was missing from the room. As I moved from group to group, I watched for her, but she was nowhere around. As soon as I could, I called this to Grant's attention.

He only laughed at my concern. "Why should you worry, Althea? At least she isn't annoying you or me."

I still wasn't convinced. Grant saw my frown and spoke more reassuringly. "Darling, we both know what a flirt she is. Don't you think it's possible she might have found a man she took a liking to. They've stepped outside for a private moment."

This was in keeping with my opinion of her. After all, I'd seen her surrounded by men all evening. She loved admiration. I nodded my head, smiling up into his eyes.

I put Helene out of my mind for the rest of the evening. I was kept busy right up until everyone began to leave. After the last guest departed, I breathed a huge sigh of relief. Then I took a look around at the sorry state of my lovely house.

"Oh dear," I wailed. "Look at this mess. And I'm so tired."

I watched the servants beginning to pick up all the discarded plates and overflowing ashtrays. Suddenly I thought of Helene. "Grant?" I called. "Where's Helene?"

He shrugged, "Gone up to bed, most likely."

I shook my head. "I haven't seen her for hours."

He chuckled, "How could you tell who was missing in this crowd?"

"I think we'd better check and see if she's upstairs," I said uneasily.

Grant looked into my face and jerked his head to Sarah. "Go look in her room," he ordered.

She ran lightly up the stairs. We heard her knock and the sound of a door opening. She leaned over the balcony to say, "Her room's empty, sir. The bed hasn't been slept in."

For the first time I saw concern on Grant's face. "When was she last seen?" he asked.

"I saw her when I went upstairs before the break for the buffet," I volunteered. "It was the same time as that silly mix-up with the ice." I turned to Sarah and said, "Do you remember what time that was?"

She looked at me blankly. "What mix-up, ma'am?"

"You sent that maid to find me," I started, but she was shaking her head.

"No, ma'am. I sent no one for you."

I looked around the room, my eyes searching for the young girl. I saw her trying to hide behind a bouquet of flowers. "You there," I called sharply. I changed my tone as I saw her shrink away from me. "Please. It's all right. You aren't in trouble," I assured her. "We need to know who sent you upstairs to find me."

She moved toward me, her face reflecting her fear. "Ma'am?" she mumbled as she curtsied.

"Who sent you to me?" I repeated. "You told me it was Sarah. Was this the lady?" I said, pointing to Sarah.

"Oh no, ma'am. The maid out by the icehouse was very pretty."

I bit at my lips. My heart fluttered in my throat. "What did she lool like?"

"She had hair the color of the sun, ma'am. She said her name was Sarah. She ordered me to go find you. She said she had seen you go upstairs. I was to tell you to come directly to the icehouse, ma'am."

"Thank you," I murmured. I turned to Grant. "Helene" was all I could say.

A search party was quickly organized. I was ordered to stay in the house, but I was too keyed up. I tagged along after Grant as he went to the barn to gather several lanterns. He had just stepped inside when I heard a clatter and his soft curse.

"What is it?" I demanded anxiously.

"Some fool left the shovel right inside the door. I tripped on it and almost broke my leg."

I didn't answer, but I felt an icy finger of dread touch my spine. I was afraid of what our search would turn up. The servants and workmen split up into groups of threes. Grant and I looked near the cemetery and that area of the bluff.

Everything had an eerie look. It was late at night and the moon was waning. Trees rustled like gentle fingers softly stirring the leaves. I walked along behind Grant, frightened and apprehensive of what was to come.

About that time we heard a shout farther down river. Grant shouted for me to go to the house, but I didn't listen. I ran after his bobbing lantern. My heart was beating wildly, keeping time with my stumbling steps.

Everyone had clustered at the top of the embankment. Their many lanterns brightened the night but cast odd shadows on the ground.

"What have you found?" demanded Grant.

"Her sir. She's dead. Down at the bottom." He pointed over the edge.

I caught my breath. I wasn't really surprised. I knew it was a possibility, but to actually hear she was dead was shocking. Grant cursed loudly and slid down the bluff, but I continued to stay where I was.

A circle of men stood around her still body but moved aside as Grant came near. Helene's long blond hair spread like a fan over the black Mississippi mud. The light from the lanterns gave her skin a glaringly white appearance. Her black gown blended in against the dark earth, leaving only her face and hair visible.

She must have tripped and fell, I told myself. She came for a walk and fell. I kept telling myself these things, but I didn't believe a word of what I was saying. I heard Grant tell Raymond to go for the sheriff.

I met Raymond as he came up the bluff. "Why the sheriff?" I demanded, my eyes searching his face for an answer.

He wouldn't meet my gaze. "She's been shot, miss. Murdered."

I felt the darkness closing in around me. Helene murdered. Why? Why her and not me? I moaned as if in pain. "Where was the danger?" I whispered. "Where was the danger?"

CHAPTER SIXTEEN

Helene's body was wrapped in a blanket and placed in the parlor. The rest of us went into the study to wait for the sheriff. We hadn't told Arthur or Celia about Helene. At this late hour we were sure they were asleep. Nothing could be done for Helene, so we let them have their rest.

Grant's face still wore that dazed expression. He moved about the room restlessly. I sat on the sofa, watching him, wishing I could find the words to comfort him. But I needed comfort myself. That question I'd asked myself out there on the bluff needed an answer. I didn't have it and I didn't know where to go to find it. I tried thinking of the party to get my mind off Helene's death, but the party had happened an eternity away, or so it seemed. What was important was Helene lying in the other room, a fatal wound in her body. Dead.

I shook my head, unable to fully grasp the significance of her death. It took the appearance of the sheriff to bring this nightmare home to me.

He took a while to view the body before coming into the study. I sat huddled in a corner of the sofa, a shawl thrown around my chilled arms. My gay dress and bright glittering jewels seemed almost disrespectful. But I hadn't wanted to go upstairs to change into something more appropriate. As it turned out, my clothes were the least of my worries.

As the sheriff came into the study, his sharp eyes rested on me briefly. "I'm sorry to keep you waiting, but I wanted to see where she was killed." He turned to me and asked, "When did you notice she was missing?"

I licked my dry lips nervously. "I think it was after the supper break. I mentioned it to Grant and we assumed she had gone outside with . . ." I stopped and felt my cheeks redden with confusion. I looked to Grant for help.

"What my wife is saying, Sheriff, is that we weren't worried. I was sure she had found someone she wanted to visit with and they had gone outside for some privacy."

"I see," he said with a faint nod of his head. "Was this a habit of hers? This picking up with just any man."

"I didn't say just any man, Sheriff," snapped Grant. "Helene wasn't a whore! She liked to be admired and fussed over. This time she picked the wrong man."

The sheriff pursed his lips thoughtfully. "You think the murderer was someone she went with willingly? When she didn't respond to his lovemaking, he shot her?"

"What else could it be?" said Grant with a shrug of his shoulders. "Who else would want to kill her?"

The sheriff turned so he could see me. "Mrs. Whitmore, how well did you and the deceased get along?"

It took me a minute to realize he was referring to Helene as "the deceased." Clearing my throat, I stammered, "Well enough." I knew that was the wrong thing to say as soon as the words left my lips.

"Did you like your mother-in-law?"

"I hardly thought of Helene as a mother-in-law," I replied without thinking.

"Really?" he asked. "How did you see her?" he said with his eyebrows raised in question.

"I don't see what this has to do with her murder," I said in confusion. "Helene and I weren't close. She's dead now. That's past."

"That's a noble thought, ma'am, except she's been killed. I have to know who her enemies were."

I leaned back with a gasp. At last I saw what he was getting at. My eyes darted nervously around the room. "My God," I breathed. "You suspect me, don't you?"

His voice was noncommittal. "I have to suspect anyone who was here and had the opportunity and motive."

"I think this has gone on long enough, Sheriff," said Grant firmly. He came to take my hand in his strong one. "My wife didn't kill anyone. She's been in the house the entire evening."

The sheriff's face was grim. "I know these questions seem unnecessary to you, but a woman was murdered here tonight. When I was here a few weeks ago, concerning the death of a man named Campbell, I heard some gossip among the servants. Now tonight I'm called back again. This time for another death. You have to realize what my position is."

"These are two separate incidents," said Grant.

"Let me be the judge," said the sheriff.

"What gossip are you referring to?" demanded Grant.

The sheriff shook his head. "I'll ask the questions, Mr. Whitmore."

"Very well," agreed Grant, but I could tell he was anything but happy. "Then get on with it. I think you're wasting your time in here with us. You should be out checking with our guests to see if anyone saw her leave the house with a man."

"What about the icehouse?" I remembered suddenly.

"What's this about the icehouse?" said the sheriff.

I quickly explained about the misunderstanding.

"What do you think she wanted you for?" he asked, his sharp eyes riveted to my face.

Now that I had brought it out, I didn't know how much to tell. I started to answer him but was interrupted by the slamming of the front door. A deputy came running into the study.

"I found something, Sheriff," he called excitedly. "I knew you'd want to see it right away."

The sheriff took one look at me and Grant and waved the young man back out into the hall. We could hear the excited voice of the deputy, followed by the deeper tone of the sheriff. Though I strained my ears, I couldn't understand what they were saying. When the sheriff came back into the study, his face revealed nothing of what he was thinking. He stood with his hands behind his back and rocked to and fro on his heels and toes. Very dramatically he held out his hand for all of us to see. But it was my face he was watching.

Quietly he said, "My deputy found something. I'm sure you remember it, Mrs. Whitmore."

Of course I remembered it. I'd never forget Campbell's gun. I'd seen it held once before just as the sheriff was handling it. It lay cradled in the palm of his hand. The light played off its silver-plated barrel.

I put a shaky hand to my throat and whispered, "Was that what killed her?"

"We're pretty sure it was," he answered. "Mrs. Whitmore?"

I had to drag my eyes away from the dreadful gun, but his voice commanded me to look at him.

"Have you been keeping this gun in your possession as a safeguard for your safety?"

"No," I said, shaking my head. I could see what he was thinking. Everything pointed to me. My hatred and my fear of Helene made me a suspect in her murder. "No," I almost whimpered, "I was afraid of her. I would never have gone out to meet her on that bluff."

"But you might have thought you were meeting someone else," persisted the sheriff.

"No" was all I could say.

"Think back to the night of Campbell's death. Did you pick up the gun later, after it was found missing?"

Grant started to interrupt, but the sheriff froze him with a glare. Softly he said, "You may stay, Mr. Whitmore, but don't interfere. I'll only take your wife into another room where I can question her privately."

I got up from the sofa. I felt vulnerable sitting. The sheriff was a large man. He towered over me, making me feel that he was already pronouncing sentence on me. Once on my feet, I soon realized I'd made a mistake. I should have stayed seated. My legs weren't strong enough to hold me. There I stood. I was able to meet the sheriff's doubting eyes, but I swayed on my feet like a drunkard.

"Well?" he snapped at me. "Did you pick the gun up that night?"

"No," I said weakly. "I couldn't bring myself to touch it. He tried to shoot Hilda with it. I was frightened."

He shook his head. His voice was rough as he said, "I'm sorry, ma'am, but I think you did. I think you've had it all this time. That's why me and my men couldn't find it."

"No," I repeated, but he didn't seem to hear me. He held the gun up to the light and said, "You know where we found this?"

He didn't wait for my answer but continued, "My deputy says down almost to the river's edge a hole has been dug. We can only guess that the body was to be dumped into the grave on top of this gun. No one walks down there, it's too steep and rough. Chances are, the grave would never have been found." His voice was low and quiet as he asked, "Is that what you had hoped?"

It came so unexpectedly that I could only stare at him blankly. I recoiled in horror at the picture he had painted with his words. I could see Helene's dainty white body being covered with that black sticky mud. I started to scream.

"I didn't kill her! I couldn't do that. She was the one after me, not me after her. Don't say any more," I pleaded. "Please."

Grant came to me, putting his arm around me. "I think that's enough, Sheriff."

"I agree," said a faint voice from the hall.

We all turned to find Aunt Celia standing in her nightgown. She was shivering almost uncontrollably. Her voice was thick with grief as she said, "Leave her be, Sheriff. If you have any more questions, ask them of me. I was there with Helene." As she spoke the name, her eyes filled with tears, but she went on with a strength I never knew she possessed. "Helene's dead. I was the one who pulled the trigger. Leave Althea alone. She's innocent."

Her words took us all by surprise. Grant went to her and guided her to a chair. He wrapped a blanket around her shoulders, at the same time saying, "Why are you doing this?"

She patted him gently on the hand. "Poor dear. For so many years, I've tried to protect everyone from my mistake and I ended up hurting you all. I killed Helene by accident, but if I hadn't she would have killed Althea."

"But why?" demanded Grant. "Althea has said all along Helene was trying to hurt her. Why?"

"I'll try to explain, my dear. I'm sure you thought you knew Helene, but I don't think any of us did. I never meant her any harm when I went outside, but she wouldn't listen to me. We fought over the gun and it went off." Celia turned to me. "I was sure it was a ploy of hers to get you away from the house with that concocted story about the ice. I couldn't let you go, my dear. I had to go instead. I found Helene waiting for you. She had the gun ready to kill you and the shovel handy to cover you up when she had finished.

"Helene had a story all ready to tell. She said she had seen you riding off with a man. She lied easily. By the time she had finished fabricating this story, everyone would have believed her. Even you, Grant. She had been planning this all week. I could see it coming. I tried to talk to her, but she brushed me aside."

I gulped away my own misery and went to the older woman.

I took her hand in mine and said, "I'm so sorry. I know you loved her very much."

Celia smiled rather sadly. "She meant more to me than I did to her. I tried so hard to tell her, but she never wanted to listen to this old woman. Then when she might have listened to me, I didn't have the courage to tell her."

"Why did she want to kill Mrs. Whitmore?" said the sheriff.

I guess we had all forgotten him, we were so concerned with Aunt Celia. She nodded to him and said, "You'll get your confession, Sheriff, but you'll have to be patient. I've kept a secret from my family for many years and it's time it came out."

She waited until we were settled, then she began to speak. Her eyes held a dreamy faraway look. I knew she was reliving the past.

"Grant, you and Nicholas were like sons to me. I adored you both. I would have done anything for you, but I had a tie to Helene too." She turned to look into Grant's eyes. "Try to understand. Don't be too hard on this old aunt of yours. What I have to say will explain many things that might have caused you to wonder over the years." She looked at me and smiled. "Even the short time you have known me, you've suspected something and tried to question me. I pushed you away then, but now I'm prepared to give all of you some answers.

"In order to understand me, you have to understand what my life was like living with my brother and his family. I was the old-maid sister. I had no one and nothing. My home was in my brother's house. I had a room. That was all. I was made to feel welcome. Whitmore Halls is big enough for several families, but it wasn't like having a home and family of my own.

"Things changed for me the day a new man came to work at the Halls. I fell in love with him. When Arthur found out, he was furious. He couldn't understand how a Whitmore could love a common laborer. Gerald was anything but common. He made me feel loved and cherished. It was a feeling I'd never experienced before or since. He was handsome and he was gentle. We could talk for hours or be content to walk along in the moonlight, not speaking. We were just happy to be together and have each other.

"I left my room at night to be with him, coming back only as dawn began. Arthur found this out by accident. I was anxious to go to Gerald, so I had left earlier than was safe. Arthur came looking for me. Finding my room empty, he made an immediate search for me. I was found in Gerald's arms. We had been making plans to run away together and be married, but Arthur wouldn't listen to us. He tossed Gerald out of the Halls. I never saw him again."

Even after so many years, the hurt was still in her eyes and heart. Celia dabbed at her tears. "I'm a foolish old woman." She laughed softly. "I waited for Gerald to come back to me, but he didn't. I hated Arthur. I wouldn't speak to him and I refused to eat. If it hadn't been for Grant's mother, I might have died. I didn't care about living. I didn't until I found I had a wonderful reason to live. Arthur might have forced Gerald from me, but I had the last laugh on my brother." Her voice was bitter. "His wonderful sister, who was much too good to marry a common worker, was about to give birth to a bastard child."

Celia glanced at Grant. "You know your father well enough to imagine his fury. He didn't give me a chance to decide what I wanted to do. He had my bags packed and literally shipped me out of his sight. He hired a nurse for me and I lived away from him in New York for the next few months. I stayed in contact with your mother, Grant. She helped me get over my feelings of being an outcast. But she couldn't give me the one thing I needed most to hear. Word of Gerald. To this day I don't know what happened to him. All the time I was carrying his child, I fantasized about him coming to New York and taking me away. We would have our child and our love. Nothing else would matter. But of course that didn't happen."

Celia was silent, her face thoughtful and soft. After a while she shook herself out of her daydreams and continued. "I had a good friend in the nurse Arthur hired for me. Her name was Francine Neilson. She knew everything about me and I trusted her with my life when it came time for the baby to be born. We didn't bother with a doctor. I was in good health and I was determined. Everything went fine. I was the mother of a tiny but very lovely baby girl."

I'd sensed where this was all heading. I suppose Grant had too. Yet to hear Celia actually say the words "I'm Helene's mother" was startling.

"Arthur expected me to give her up, but I couldn't let her go to strangers I didn't know anything about. Instead I paid Francine to keep her. She was to raise Helene as her own. I bought her a house and I went back to the Halls and to my brother, who didn't want to face me. I could read the shame for me in his eyes. I was so lonely. All I had were memories. It helped to get letters from Francine. They came to a dear friend of mine in town. I lived for those letters telling me of Helene's growth and progress.

"Finally I could stand it no longer. I wanted my daughter closer to me. I wanted her near enough so that I could see her as often as I wanted. I sent money to Francine and told her to move to New Orleans. Francine's health wasn't very good. She was glad to make the move. I never breathed a word of their existence to anyone. I was afraid word might leak back to Arthur. Years ago he had forbidden me to speak of the child and of Gerald.

"I found a lovely young woman in Helene. She was seventeen years old and so beautiful. It was hard to keep my hands off her. I wanted to hold her and tell her she was my little girl, but I didn't. I remained her kindly Aunt Celia, a friend of her mother's. Helene loved living in New Orleans. She liked the excitement of a new town and she had a throng of admirers."

Celia shook her head. "I think the hardest thing to accept in seeing Helene every day was to see how Francine had spoiled her. Helene was so willful and conceited. She took my regular visits for granted. But she didn't care if she saw me, it was the packages I always brought her. Helene was so demanding. I tried to speak to Francine about it, but she brushed my worries aside. I forgot about everything else when I found out that Helene's most persistent suitor was my own nephew, Nicholas."

Celia closed her eyes and rocked back and forth, hugging her stomach as if in pain. "My God, how I cried the day he came to me and said he and Helene were getting married. I tried to tell him he couldn't marry her. I even threatened to cut him out of my will, but he loved her. Nothing I said could change their minds. I didn't have Francine to help me discourage them. She had died about a year before that. Helene was alone, which made her all the more vulnerable. Faced with so much opposition, they ran away and got married." Celia shook her head. "I was out of my mind. I didn't know what to do or who to turn to. In their note Nicholas said they would be back at the Halls in a few days. They were seeking privacy at Helene's cottage for a while."

She rocked back and forth, hugging herself tightly. "God, but I wish I had my life to do over again. I went to the cottage as soon as I read the note. I couldn't let them love each other. A child born of their marriage might . . ." She gulped noisily. "I couldn't bear thinking of it. They had to be told right away. I needed time to plan what I wanted to say, so I tied my buggy down the lane and walked the rest of the way."

Celia stopped to look at Grant, then quickly away. "I hadn't walked far when I heard a horse approaching. I ducked into the hedge at the side of the road. When I saw it was Nicholas, I came out of hiding. My sudden appearance startled the horse. He bucked once then started to run. Nicholas, taken by surprise, was thrown off. When I got to him, he was already dead." She covered her face with her hands. Her voice was muffled. "God forgive me my deceit. It has brought nothing but pain and death."

I forgot her to turn to Grant. I knew how much he loved his brother and how much he loved his aunt. I saw his jaw set grimly. His frosty blue eyes stared off into space. As Celia began to speak again, I turned back to her. I would comfort Grant later. He would need me more than ever, I was sure.

"I thought it was all over with Nicholas' death. Helene was a bride and a widow all in one day. I could have told all of you what had happened, but I didn't think it mattered. Nicholas was gone and I couldn't face your hatred for me. So I kept quiet. I was sure Helene would find another man to love. I never dreamed she would come back to the Halls. And you, Grant," Celia sighed, wiping her eyes. "My other nephew fell victim to her charms as well.

"I could see you were infatuated with her. I had to do something. I wasn't going to let anything happen to you. I was ready to go to Arthur when the two of you argued and you had your accident. I saw Helene's squeamishness toward your injury. I emphasized it, making it much worse than it was. I told her how miserable her life would be, married to a cripple." Celia held out her hands to Grant. Her eyes beseeched him to forgive her and to understand.

"I knew you were hurt by her attitude. Helene was easy to influence and it was one way out for all of us. When you went away, I knew you were bitter, but I was sure you would find someone better suited for you than Helene." Her eyes touched me tenderly. "I was right. Althea is just the right person for you."

I looked at her blue lips and trembling hands. I said, "That's enough for tonight. Why don't you rest now? Anything else you have to say can wait until morning."

"No!" she said stoutly, squaring her shoulders. "I've kept it in too long now. You have to hear it all. I'm not going to try to minimize my part in this. It's my fault. I thought marriage to

Arthur would be a good thing. Both my nephews were gone from the Halls. I still loved Helene and wanted her near me, especially now that I was growing old. I urged her to accept Arthur's proposal. He had no use for a wife as far as husbandly duties were concerned, but he did need someone to run the house and play hostess at any dinner he gave. Everything worked out for a while, but Helene became more and more unhappy. She wanted the name, the money and the recognition, but she wanted the excitement and romance as well. Arthur wasn't prepared to give her that. When we heard Grant had married, she was unfit to live with. She pleaded and badgered Arthur into making this trip. He didn't need much persuasion. He wanted to see what would cause his only remaining son to turn his back on his birthplace."

Her sad gaze moved from Grant to me and back to Grant again. "This has been difficult to talk about, but it did happen a long time ago. However, what I have to say now has been happening recently. I've tried to explain how Helene was raised so you might understand her nature better. She could be cruel. She was very spoiled. When we came and she saw Grant and how healthy and handsome he was, she was furious with me for talking her out of marriage to him years ago. It didn't matter that he was happily married. She decided to take what she had always wanted. At first I was able to convince myself that Althea's falls were accidents. Then I accepted the fact that Helene meant you great harm, my dear. I tried to talk to her, but she only laughed at me. It was the evening of that terrible rainstorm that I sensed a change in her. I could see wanting Grant was only secondary to her hatred for you. She wanted you dead."

Celia shivered. "That's the first time I've said those words aloud. It's hard to use them in reference to Helene, but I know they are true. She watched your love for each other and knew that she was tied to an old man who was paralyzed. She was jealous of you, Althea. Jealous of your happiness. I watched her spying on you. I wanted to warn you, but I didn't know what I could say. It all needed to come out, but I lacked the courage. I prayed this party of yours would make her forget about you."

She leaned down to touch my hand lightly. In an apologetic manner, she whispered, "I destroyed your lovely gown."

"But why?" I said in surprise. I'd never dreamed it was she.

She sighed deeply. "How do I explain what was in my mind? I thought it might work as a warning to you but most of all to Grant. I wanted him to help protect you. Helene had such an air of excitement about her that I knew the night of the party was when she was going to make her move. She was obsessed with the thought of killing you. That night when Mr. Campbell died, I saw her pick up something near the front porch. She tucked it under her cape. I asked her what she had found, but she ignored me. Tonight I found out what it was. The gun that had been lost. She was fascinated by it."

Celia turned to the sheriff. "I'm sure none of this has interested you up until now. I'm ready to tell you about her death. You see, I knew she was expecting Althea to come to the icehouse. When I went instead, it threw her into a rage. She waved the gun around, threatening me. I told her to stop acting like a spoiled child, but this was an entirely different Helene. It was as if she was out of touch with reality. She wanted Althea. I spoke softly to her, trying to quiet her, but she was past listening to me. She wanted to try out the gun, she said. She wanted to see if those cute little bullets could really kill. She urged me out to the bluffs."

Celia's face crumpled. Her hurt went deep. "I knew then that she didn't care what happened to me. She was going to kill me. Her own mother. I was in her way. I played along with her until we were almost to the embankment. It was then I made a grab for the gun. She tried to move out of my reach, but I had caught her off guard. She hadn't expected me to resist her. All her life I'd been there to give and give. Now she was seeing another side of me. I was trying to take it away from her when it discharged."

Celia shut her eyes painfully. "Her beautiful face softened. She looked up at me, unable to believe what had happened. Then she said, 'I thought you would stand by me.'" Celia drew a shuddering breath. "I tried to catch her as she fell, but she slipped away and rolled down the incline. I stood there waiting for her to get up and start shouting at me, but she lay still."

Her voice rose hysterically. "This wasn't the way it was supposed to end! I was the culprit, the villain. I have made so many people pay for my mistakes. I couldn't leave her alone. I scrambled down the embankment, hoping she was just unconscious, but I saw at once she wasn't breathing. By the light of the moon, I saw the grave she had dug. I knew Helene had planned to put Althea there. I was appalled by what she had in mind. I thought to bury Helene there instead, but I couldn't bring myself to cover my only child with that horrible smelly mud. Sick to my stomach, I went back to the house. I didn't care what happened next, not until I heard voices down here. I came to the head of the stairs and heard the sheriff accusing Althea. I couldn't let her pay too. That was when I came to a decision that should have been made years ago. My story had to be told." She leaned back wearily in her chair.

Everything had been explained except for one simple thing. I asked, "Why did you take the shovel back to the barn?"

She gave a short laugh. "I really don't know, my dear. It was lying beside Helene. I used it like a cane to get back up the bluff. My mind wasn't working very normally. When I got to the top, I kept walking on to the barn." She closed her eyes.

We were all silent. I watched Grant and the sheriff leave the room. Celia didn't open her eyes. She sat with her back ramrod stiff. It was as if a huge weight had been rolled from her shoulders. Her tears were gone. She seemed almost relaxed. I knew she was exhausted. I hoped she would be allowed to rest.

I eased my hand out of hers and paced the floor restlessly. I thought back over her words. Poor, poor woman. It couldn't have been an easy time for her. Pride. Such a small word to describe so many big problems. If Arthur had only shown more compassion toward Celia. But no, I couldn't put all the blame on the old man. Celia could have spoken up for her love and her child. She could have shown more courage. Arthur had been the domineering force in her life. It had taken great courage to tell everything now. I was sorry she hadn't found the strength long ago. I looked back at her face. I saw only peace and calm where moments ago it had been ravaged with torment and remembrance.

I turned from studying Celia to watch Grant come back into the room. He went to his aunt, kneeling at her side.

"Come, Auntie. Let's go upstairs. You need your rest."

She shivered, then opened her eyes slowly. A sweet smile stole across her lips. She put a hand on Grant's dark curly head. "My, boy, you should be in bed yourself. Tomorrow, Nicholas, we go to the county fair." She smiled widely. "I haven't forgotten my promise, child."

Grant's face registered his surprise and concern, but he kept his voice firm. "It's me. Grant. Come with me."

She clicked her tongue in disapproval. "Darling, Grant's away. I know you miss him, but he'll be home soon."

I saw Grant start to correct her, but he stopped. "Come with me," he repeated softly as he helped her come slowly to her feet.

Celia looked around her, blinking in confusion. "Where are we, Nicholas? Is this the Halls?"

"No," whispered Grant, his voice thick with grief. "This is Willowcrest. You and Father have come to visit, remember?"

She looked around her, shaking her head. "It's all so lovely. I'd like to live in a home like this, Nicholas. It's so bright and pretty. Not like the Halls. The Halls never change. It looks just like it did when your grandfather was alive."

"I know," he choked. "Come, let me take your arm."

Her shoulders sagged wearily. "Yes, dear. Take me to my room. Suddenly I feel so tired," she mumbled, "so tired."

I wiped the tears away with the back of my hand. "What will happen now?" I asked the sheriff.

He looked contrite. "She's erased this entire evening from her mind. She's gone back to a time in her life before all the trouble started."

"She won't have to go to jail, will she?" I asked.

"No," he said, shaking his head. He looked at me and added, "I have to apologize for the way I questioned you earlier. I got off on the wrong track. I'm sorry, Mrs. Whitmore."

I waved away his apology. "It doesn't matter now. If you'll excuse me, I want to go to Grant. He might need some help." I hurried from the study. In the upstairs hall, I found Grant coming out of Celia's room.

He put an arm around me. We drew strength from each other.

"I can't take it all in, Althea," he murmured. "She was Helene's mother and none of us had any idea at all." He shook his head. "My God, can you imagine the pain and the suffering she's had to endure all these years?"

"I know," I sighed. "Is she all right?"

"Who's to say? She isn't in any pain. Right now she's probably happier than she's been in years. She's living in the past. Back to a time when Nicholas and I were just children. Sarah's with her, helping her get ready for bed."

Grant laughed remorsefully. "It's like a terrible nightmare. I keep thinking I'll wake up and find it was just a dream."

But we knew it wasn't. Arthur had to be told. Together Grant and I would look after him and Celia. I felt the warmth of my husband's arm around me. Bitterness was gone. I knew that during our married life we would have to weather many more storms. This was just our first. Together our love would make us strong.

I tightened my grip on Grant's neck, pulling his head down

to mine. I looked up into his sad eyes and smiled tenderly. No words were needed. He knew I loved him, just as I knew his love for me was firm and true.

With our arms wrapped around each other, we stood in the hall of Willowcrest, watching the dawn of a new day begin. We didn't know what it would bring, but together we would see it through.